Bernhard Schlink was born in Germany in 1944. A professor of law at Humboldt University, Berlin, and Cardozo Law School, New York, he is the author of the major international bestselling novel *The Reader*, made into an Oscar-winning film, and the short-story collection *Flights of Love*, as well as several prize-winning crime novels. He lives in Berlin and New York.

By Bernhard Schlink

The Gordian Knot

BERNHARD SCHLINK

TRANSLATED FROM THE GERMAN BY
PETER CONSTANTINE

PHOENIX

A PHOENIX PAPERBACK

First published in Great Britain in 2011
by Weidenfeld & Nicolson
This paperback edition published in 2012
by Phoenix,
an imprint of Orion Books Ltd,
Orion House, 5 Upper St Martin's Lane,
London WC2H 9EA

An Hachette UK company

1 3 5 7 9 10 8 6 4 2

Originally published in Switzerland as *Die Gordische Schleife*
By Diogenes Verlag AG, Zürich, in 1988

Copyright © Bernhard Schlink 1988
Translation copyright © Peter Constantine 2010

This edition published by arrangement with Pantheon Books,
a division of Random House, Inc.

The right of Bernhard Schlink and Peter Constantine to be identified
as the author and translator of this work respectively has been asserted
by them in accordance with the Copyright, Designs and Patents Act 1988.

Grateful acknowledgement is made to Walter Popp for his
consultation on the translation.

A CIP catalogue record for this book
is available from the British Library.

ISBN 978-0-7538-2846-5

Printed and bound in Great Britain by
Clays Ltd, St Ives plc

The Orion Publishing Group's policy is to use papers that
are natural, renewable and recyclable products and
made from wood grown in sustainable forests. The logging
and manufacturing processes are expected to conform to
the environmental regulations of the country of origin.

www.orionbooks.co.uk

The Gordian Knot

Part One

I

GEORG WAS DRIVING HOME. He left the highway by Aix and took a back road. From Marseille to Aix there are no tolls, from Aix to Pertuis there is a charge of five francs: that's a pack of Gauloises.

Georg lit one. The trip to Marseille hadn't panned out. The head of the translation agency that sent him jobs now and then had had no work for him this time. "I said I'd give you a call if anything came up. Things are a bit slow right now." Monsieur Maurin had assumed an anxious expression—what he had said might in fact be true. It was his agency, but he lived off jobs from the aircraft factory in Toulon, the Industries Aéronautiques Mermoz. When the joint European venture for a new fighter-helicopter in which Mermoz was involved stalled, there was nothing for Monsieur Maurin to translate. Or else he had once again tried to get better terms and Mermoz was teaching him a lesson. Or the factory had made good its long-standing threat and hired its own translators.

The road rose steeply beyond Aix, and the engine stuttered. Georg broke out in a sweat. This was all he needed! He had bought the old Peugeot only three weeks ago—his parents had come to visit him from Heidelberg and given him the money. "I think you really need a car for your job," his father had said, and dropped two thousand marks in the box on the kitchen counter in which Georg kept his money. "You know Mother and I like to help all we can. But now that I'm retired and your sister has a baby . . ."

Then came the questions Georg had heard a thousand times: Couldn't he find himself a better job nearer home? Why had he left his job as a lawyer in Karlsruhe? Couldn't he come back to Germany now that he'd broken up with Hanne? Was he going to abandon his parents in their old age? There was more to life, after all, than finding oneself. "Do you want your mother to die all alone?" Georg was ashamed, because he was happy enough for the two thousand marks, but didn't care in the least what his father was saying.

The gas tank was almost full, and he had changed the oil and filter not too long ago, so there couldn't be anything wrong. As he drove on, he listened to the engine the way a mother listens to the breath of a feverish child. The car wasn't jerking anymore. But wasn't there some kind of thumping? A grinding, crunching noise? Georg had driven the car for three weeks without experiencing any problems. Now there was that noise again.

At noon Georg parked in Pertuis, did some shopping at the market, and had a beer at a pub. It was the beginning of March; the tourists hadn't yet arrived. The stall with herbs of Provence, honey, soap, and lavender water—swamped during the summer months by Germans and Americans until late in the afternoon—had already been taken down. In other stalls, the merchandise was being put away. The air was warm and there were heavy clouds. A gust of wind rattled the awnings. It smelled of rain.

Georg leaned against the wall near the entrance of the bar, glass in hand. He was wearing jeans, a frayed brown leather jacket over a

blue sweater, and a dark cap. His posture was relaxed; from a distance he could have passed for a young farmer who had finished
his business at the market and was now unwinding before lunch.
Close up, his face showed hard lines on his forehead and around
his mouth, a deep groove in his chin, and a nervous fatigue around
the eyes. He took his cap off and ran his hand over his hair. It had
gotten thin. He had aged in the last couple of years. Before, he had
had a beard and could have been anywhere between twenty-five
and forty. Now one could see his thirty-eight years, and might perhaps guess him older.

The first raindrops fell. Georg went inside, and bumped into
Maurice, Yves, Nadine, Gérard, and Catrine. They too were
struggling to get by, taking on odd jobs, living off wife or girlfriend, husband or boyfriend. Gérard and Catrine were managing
best: he had a small restaurant in Cucuron, and she was working in
a bookstore in Aix. Outside, the rain was drumming, and as they
ordered round after round of pastis, Georg began to feel better. He
would make it. They would all make it. In any case, it had been
two years since he had left Karlsruhe. He had survived. And he had
also survived splitting up with Hanne.

As Georg drove up into the mountains bordering the valley of
Durance to the north, the sun broke through. The view opened
out on to a broad valley with vineyards, orchards, vegetable fields,
a pond, and single farms, with the mountains of Luberon dimin-
ishing toward the south. There were a few small towns not much
bigger than villages, but they all had castles, cathedrals, or the ruins
of fortresses: the kind of miniature world one dreams of as a child
and builds with toy blocks. Georg loved this view in the fall and
winter too, when the land lies brown and smoke drifts over the
fields, or rises from chimneys. Now he was enjoying the green of
spring and the light of summer. The sun flashed on the pond and

the greenhouses. Ansouis appeared, a defiant little town on a lonely rise. A road lined with cypress trees led to a high stone bridge and a castle. Georg drove under the bridge, turned right, and a few miles later, right again onto an overgrown gravel path. His house lay by the fields outside Cucuron.

2

GEORG AND HANNE HAD MOVED in together two years ago. His departure from Karlsruhe had been problematic: a quarrel with his boss at the law firm, recriminations and tears from Hanne's ex-boyfriend, a fight with his parents, and a nagging fear that he was burning all his bridges. What should have been a liberating escape had almost become an all-out flight. Georg and Hanne couldn't find work in Paris, where they had first wanted to settle down. They lived in a run-down tenement, and their relationship seemed to be at an end. Cucuron offered them a new beginning. Georg had fallen in love with the little town on a vacation, and he was hoping he would find a job in Aix or Avignon. The first few weeks were bad. But then Georg got a part-time job as a projectionist in Avignon, and they had found the house.

They were pleased that their new home lay on a southern slope, isolated, surrounded by cherry and plum trees and melon and tomato fields; they loved that their garden and balcony had sun from dawn to dusk, and that it was shady and cool beneath the balcony that ran the whole length of the second floor. There was a lot of space, with two rooms downstairs and three upstairs, and an addition to the house that Hanne could use as a studio. She sketched and painted.

They brought over their furniture and Hanne's easel from Karlsruhe. Georg planted an herb garden, and Hanne set up her studio. When he was no longer needed at the cinema, Hanne got herself a part-time job at a printer's. In the harvest season they both worked as field hands. In the winter Georg got his first translation jobs from Monsieur Maurin. But try as they might they couldn't make ends meet, and she went back to Karlsruhe to stay with her parents for two months. They were wealthy, and happy to support their daughter—as long as she wasn't in Paris or Cucuron, and as long as she wasn't living with Georg. Two months turned into four. She only came back over Christmas, and then one more time to collect her belongings. Her new boyfriend was sitting at the wheel of the van into which she loaded the cabinet, bed, table, chair, fourteen boxes, and her easel. Hanne left Georg the two cats.

When he was twenty-five Georg had married Steffi, his high school sweetheart from Heidelberg. By thirty he was divorced, and over the next few years had various girlfriends for shorter or longer periods. At thirty-five he had met Hanne, and was convinced that she was the one for him.

He liked deliberating: about high school sweethearts marrying; lawyers in partnership; smokers and nonsmokers; doers and ponderers; natural and artificial intelligence; adjusting to circumstances or turning one's back on them; about the right kind of life. He particularly liked theorizing about relationships: whether it was better for both parties to fall head over heels in love, or for love to develop gradually; whether relationships evolved the way they began or whether profound changes were possible; whether they demonstrated their quality by lasting or to some extent fulfilling themselves and coming to an end; whether there was such a thing in life as the right woman or the right man, or whether one simply lived different lives with different people; whether it is best for both partners to be alike or not.

In theory, Hanne *was* the right partner for him. She was very different. She wasn't intellectual and abstract, but spontaneous and direct, a wonderful lover, and also stimulating and independent when it came to planning their projects. She helps me do everything I've always wanted to do but didn't dare, he thought.

Now, alone with two cats in a house that was too large and too expensive, and a book project that had ground to a halt in its early phase in which he was to write the story and she to illustrate it, Georg lost his taste for theorizing. Hanne had left him in February—the coldest February any of the neighbors could recall—and Georg often had no idea where he would find the money to heat the house. There were times he would have liked to talk everything over with her, to figure out why their relationship had floundered, but she never answered his letters, and his phone had been cut off.

He made it through the rest of the winter and the following year. Perhaps he could eke out a living with the translation jobs Monsieur Maurin might send. But there was no relying on when or if these jobs would materialize. He sent out a flurry of letters, soliciting literary translations, technical translations, offering French lawyers his German legal expertise, and German newspapers reports and articles from Provence. All to no avail. That he now had more than enough leisure time didn't help either.

In his mind there were endless feature articles, short stories, and mystery novels that he would have liked to write. But the strongest element was fear. When might Monsieur Maurin call again? Or when should I call him? Maurin had told me the day after tomorrow, but what if he has a job for me tomorrow and can't get in touch with me? Will he give the job to someone else? Should I call him tomorrow after all?

Like all despondent people, Georg became irritable. As if the world owed him something, and he had to speak up. Sometimes he was more at odds with the world, sometimes less: less, when he had written letters to potential employers and taken them to the post office, irresistible letters; or when he had completed an assignment, had money in his pocket, and was hanging out at Gérard's restaurant, Les Vieux Temps; or when he ran into people who were struggling as much as he was, but not giving up hope; or when there was a nice fire in the fireplace and the house smelled of the lavender he had picked in the fields and had hung from the mantle; or when he had visitors from Germany, real visitors, not just people who were using his place as a rest stop on their way to Spain; or when he had an idea for a story, or came home and his mailbox was filled with letters. No, he wasn't always despondent and irritable. In the fall the neighbors' cat had a litter, and Georg acquired a small black tomcat with white paws. Dopey. His other two cats were called Snow White and Sneezy. Snow White was a tomcat too, all white.

When Georg arrived home from Marseille and got out of the car, the cats rubbed against his legs. They caught plenty of mice in the fields and brought him the mice, but what they really wanted was food out of a can.

"Hi there, cats. I'm back. No work for me, I'm afraid. Not today and not tomorrow. You're not interested? You don't mind? Snow White, you're a big cat, old enough to understand that without work there's no food. As for you, Dopey, you're a silly little kitten who doesn't know anything yet." Georg picked him up and went over to the mailbox. "Take a look at that, Dopey. We got a nice fat letter, sent by a nice fat publisher. What we need is for there to be a nice fat bit of news for us in that envelope."

He unlocked the front door, which was also the kitchen door. In the refrigerator there was a half-empty can of cat food and a half-empty bottle of white wine. He fed the cats and poured himself a glass, put on some music, opened the door that led from the living room onto the terrace, and took the glass and the envelope over to the rocking chair. All the while he continued talking to the cats and to himself. Over the past year it had become a habit. "The envelope can wait a bit. It won't run away. Have you cats ever seen an envelope running? Or an envelope that minds waiting? If there's good news inside, then the wine should be at hand for a celebration—and if it's bad news, as a consolation."

Georg had read a French novel he'd liked that hadn't yet been translated into German. A novel that had the makings of a best seller and cult book. A novel that fit perfectly in that specific publisher's list. Georg had sent them the book and a sample translation.

> Dear Herr Polger,
> Thank you for your letter of . . . It was with great interest
> that we read . . . We are as enthusiastic as you are . . .
> indeed fits our list . . . we have negotiated the rights with
> Flavigny . . . As for your proposal to translate this work, we
> regret to inform you that our long-term relationship with
> our in-house translator . . . We are returning your
> manuscript . . . Sincerely . . .

"The damn bastards! They snatched my idea and sent me packing. They don't even feel the need to pay me, or offer me another job, or at least something in the future. For two weeks I sat over that sample—two whole weeks for nothing! The damn bastards!"

He got up and gave the watering can a kick.

3

DEBTS, GEORG DELIBERATED, ARE very much like the weather: I might be driving to Marseille, leave here in bright sunshine, and arrive there in the pouring rain; on the way there's the odd cloud over Pertuis, a thick cloud cover over Aix, and by Cabriès the first raindrops fall. On the other hand, I might be sitting here on my terrace: first the sun is shining in a clear blue sky, then a cloud or two appears, then more, then it starts drizzling, and finally it pours. In both cases it's a matter of an hour—an hour in the car, or an hour on my terrace, and for me the result is the same whether I drive from good weather into bad, or stay where I am and the weather turns bad. The clouds look no different, and either way I get wet. And then my parents and friends warn me not to get any deeper into debt! Not that they're wrong. Sometimes I do things that make me go deeper into debt. But all too often the debts grow into a mountain that keeps on rising. But how they grow is of no consequence to me. The result is the same.

Georg had just come home from dining at Gérard's Les Vieux Temps. He had a tab running there, but usually paid up. When he finished a job and had some money, he'd even leave a bit extra. But how petty people could be, Georg thought angrily. He'd gone to

Les Vieux Temps after receiving the disappointing letter, and Gérard had served him salmon fettuccine along with wine, coffee, and Calvados. When Gérard brought the check he didn't refuse to put it on the tab, but he made a face and dropped a hint. Georg couldn't let that pass. He paid up in full on the spot, and then some. Even though it was the money with which he was intending to pay his phone bill.

The following morning he began cleaning up the studio. He had ordered some firewood to be delivered in the afternoon, and he wanted to store it there. The wood was ordered and, luckily, already paid for. He couldn't recall the foolish impulse that had led him to place the order. There was more than enough wood lying about in the woods of Cucuron.

Georg didn't like going into the studio. The memory of Hanne was especially present and painful. Her large desk by the window, which they had assembled together and on which they had made love by way of inauguration and to test its sturdiness. The sketches for her last big oil painting hung on the wall, and the smock she had left behind was hanging on a hook. Because the boiler and the boxes of books were in the studio, he couldn't avoid going there altogether, but he had neglected it.

He wanted to do something about the studio, but didn't get very far. By the time he finished, the boxes of books were stacked up, there was space for the firewood, and Hanne's smock was in the trash. But then what did he need the studio for?

A car pulled up outside, but it wasn't the wood being delivered or the mail. It was Herbert, another German living in Pertuis, whose aim in life was to paint, but who always seemed to be kept from doing so by things coming up. They had a bottle of wine together and talked about this and that. Mostly about the latest things that had come up.

"By the way," Herbert said as he was leaving, "can you help me out with a loan of five hundred francs? You see, there's this gallery in Aix, and . . ."

"Five hundred? I'm sorry, but I don't have that kind of money," Georg replied with a shrug, holding up his empty hands.

"I thought we were friends!" Herbert said angrily.

"Even if you were my own brother, I couldn't give you anything—I don't have anything."

"I bet you have enough to pay for the next bottle of wine and the next month's rent. At least you could be decent enough to say you don't want to give me the money!"

The truck delivering the firewood arrived. It was a scratched and dented pickup with an open bed, the doors of the cab missing. A man and a woman got out, both quite old. The man had only one arm.

"Where would Monsieur like us to stack the wood? It's good wood, dry and aromatic. We collected it over there." The man waved his one arm toward the slopes of the Luberon.

"You're such a lying asshole!" Herbert said, got in his car, and drove off.

The old couple wouldn't let Georg unload the wood himself. He couldn't keep the old woman from dragging it to the edge of the truck bed, or the man from stacking it up in the studio. Georg kept hurrying with armfuls of wood from her to him.

At lunchtime he drove to Cucuron. The town is spread out over two adjacent hills, one crowned with a church, the other with the ruins of a castle. The old wall still winds around half the town, houses leaning against it. The positive feeling Georg had had many years ago when he first visited Cucuron returned whenever he went rattling through its lanes in his car, and even more whenever he set out on a half-hour walk through the fields and the town came into view—ocher-colored in the shining sun, or gray as it hid under low-hanging clouds—always stolid, cozy, reliable.

The *étang* lies in front of the town gate, a large, walled pond, rectangular and surrounded by old plane trees. On the narrow side facing the town lies the market and the Bar de l'Étang, with tables set up on the sidewalk from spring to fall. In the summer it's cool, and in the fall the plane trees drop their leaves early enough so one can sit outside in the last warm rays of the sun. This place was cozy too. In the bar they served sandwiches and draft beer, and everyone Georg knew would get together here.

This time Georg found that even with his third beer contentment didn't set in. He was still angry about Gérard and Herbert. Angry about the whole miserable situation. He drove home and took a nap. Will I end up like Herbert, or am I already there?

At four o'clock the phone woke him up. "I'm calling from Bulnakov Translation Service. Is this Monsieur Polger?"

"Yes."

"A few weeks ago we opened a translation agency in Cadenet, and business has picked up faster than we expected. We're looking for translators, and you came to our attention. Are you available?"

Georg was now wide awake. Only his voice was still unsteady. "You would like me to . . . I mean, if I'm available, to work . . . ? Yes, I believe I am."

"Great. We're at rue d'Amazone, right across the square where the statue of the drummer boy is—you'll see the sign on the building. Why don't you stop by?"

4

GEORG WAS READY TO GO THERE RIGHT AWAY. But he stopped himself. He also stopped himself on Wednesday and Thursday. He decided to go to the Bulnakov Translation Service on Friday morning at ten. Jeans, blue shirt, and leather jacket, a folder under his arm with samples of the work he had done for Monsieur Maurin: he carefully choreographed the scene—he would show that he was interested in working for them, but wouldn't indicate how much depended on it.

Everything went smoothly. Georg called on Friday morning and made an appointment for ten. He parked on the square near the statue of the drummer boy, walked up the rue d'Amazone, and at five past ten rang the bell beneath the plaque that said BULNAKOV TRANSLATION SERVICE.

The door on the third floor was open. There was the smell of paint, and a young woman was sitting at her typewriter in the freshly painted reception area. Brown hair hanging to her shoulders, brown eyes, and, as she looked up, a friendly glance and the hint of a smile.

"Monsieur Polger? Please take a seat. Monsieur Bulnakov will see you right away."

She said *Polgé* and *Boulnakóv,* but with an accent Georg couldn't quite place.

He had barely sat down on one of the brand-new chairs when a door flew open and Bulnakov, all effervescence and affability, came bursting into the room, ruddy-cheeked and sporting a tight vest and loud tie.

"How wonderful that fate has brought you to our doorstep, my young friend. May I call you 'my young friend'? We've gotten so many jobs we can barely keep up with them, and I see you're carrying a big folder of work that you are toiling over—but no, a young man like you wouldn't be *toiling*—I'm sure you can do these translation jobs with a flick of the wrist. You're young, just as I was once, correct me if I'm wrong!" He was holding Georg's hand in both of his, squeezing it, shaking it, not letting go even after he had dragged Georg into his office.

"Monsieur Bulnakov . . ."

"Let me close the door to my *sanctum,* and speak a few words of introduction—oh, what the hell, let us segue in medias res without further ado. What we do here is technical translation: handbooks for word processing, bookkeeping, systems for client- and customer-tracking, and so on. Small, convenient, friendly programs, but nice thick books. Know what I mean? I take it you have experience with technology and computers, that you can handle both English into French and French into English, and that you can work fast? Working fast is the be-all and end-all in this business, and if your dictaphone and ours aren't compatible, we'll provide you with one. Mademoiselle Kramsky will type everything up, you'll give it a quick once-over, and voilà! *Cito cito:* wasn't that the motto of your Frederick the Great? You're German, aren't you? Although, now that I think of it, the motto might not have been your Frederick the Great's but our Peter the Great's. Anyway, who cares, same difference. You haven't said a word, is anything wrong?"

Bulnakov released Georg's hand and closed the door. Here in his office there was also the smell of fresh paint, and a new desk, a new chair, a new seating area, and along the wall two built-in niches piled high with folders. Above them technical drawings were pinned to the wall with thumbtacks. Bulnakov stood in front of his desk looking at Georg with benevolence and concern, and asked again, "Is anything wrong? Is it what we pay that's making you hesitate? Ah, I know it's a touchy subject, believe you me, but I can't afford to pay more than thirty-five centimes a word. Not the kind of money that will make anyone rich—no Croesus, but no Diogenes either. Not that I'm saying you're a Diogenes, it's just a manner of speaking."

Thirty-five centimes a word—Maurin was paying him that, but only now that he'd been working for him half a year. Not to mention that he would no longer have to drive all the way to Marseille, nor would he have to do the typing himself.

"I'm very grateful for your kind words, Monsieur, and that you are interested in my working for you," Georg said. "I would gladly fit any jobs you care to give me into my schedule, and in fact keep my schedule open, but I charge fifty centimes. You might wish to consider this and give me a call, but as of now it seems that your expectations and mine do not coincide."

What a stilted answer, but Georg was pleased with it and proud he wasn't selling himself cheap. And to hell with it if it didn't work out.

Bulnakov laughed. "I see you're a man who knows his worth, a man who demands his price! I like that, my young friend, I like it very much. May I propose forty-five centimes? Let's shake on it! Shall we do business?"

Georg was handed an envelope with the galley pages of a handbook. "The first half is due next Monday, and the rest on Wednesday. Also, there's an IBM conference in Lyon next Thursday and

Friday. If you could go there with Mademoiselle Kramsky as our representative, and keep your ears to the ground and your pen at the ready, jotting down whatever people say, we would pay a thousand francs a day plus expenses. As far as those fees go, they're nonnegotiable—no ifs, ands, or buts. Agreed? You must excuse me now."

Georg spoke with Mademoiselle Kramsky about the trip. He hadn't noticed before that she was pretty—or now his good mood made her seem so. A white blouse with white embroidery, white edging above her breasts, and short sleeves, one rolled up, the other unbuttoned. She wasn't wearing a bra, had small, firm breasts, and golden hairs shimmered on her tanned arms. Her collar was round, pretty, and the top buttons coquettishly undone, and when she laughed her eyes laughed too. By her right eyebrow, beside her nose, she had a small trembling dimple while she was thinking: Should we go by train or car, and when should we start, Wednesday evening perhaps, after we're finished with the typing and proofreading of the handbook. Georg made a joke; a thick ray of sunlight fell between the two church towers outside the window, and in its light Mademoiselle Kramsky shook her head laughing, sparks dancing in her hair.

5

GEORG HAD NEVER WORKED AS HARD AS he did on the following days—not for his state examination, and not as a lawyer. This wasn't just because the handbook was thick and he found translating English computer language into French rather difficult, nor was it in anticipation of the next job they would give him, or the ones after that with all the money they would bring. He was bursting with energy and wanted to show what he was capable of: to himself, to Bulnakov, and to the world. Saturday evening he ate at Gérard's, and after his coffee went back home without first having his usual glass of Calvados. Sunday morning he took a short walk, but only because he preferred thinking about the HELP-function while walking rather than at his desk; otherwise, he sat in his room or on the terrace and even forgot to smoke. By Monday morning he had translated and dictated two-thirds of the handbook. He drove to Cadenet whistling, singing, and beating the rhythm on the steering wheel. He met neither Monsieur Bulnakov nor Mademoiselle Kramsky, but gave the cassette to a young man who barely opened his mouth to utter "*merci*," and went back home to finish the translation. By Tuesday evening it was done. Wednesday morning he breakfasted on the balcony—bacon and eggs, freshly baked bread, orange juice, and coffee, while he let the sun's rays warm his back. He listened to the cicadas and the birds, smelled the lavender, and looked over the green countryside to Ansouis, whose castle towered out of the mist. He packed his suit for the conference, and was in Cadenet by ten.

Monsieur Bulnakov's plump red face was beaming. "The translation is very good, my young friend, very good indeed. I've already looked through it—you needn't bother going over it again. How about joining me for a cup of coffee? Mademoiselle Kramsky will be here any minute, and then the two of you can head out."

"What about the last part of the handbook?"

"Mademoiselle Kramsky's colleague will type it and I'll edit it. As long as you get to Lyon as quickly as possible. You mustn't miss the mayor's reception."

Monsieur Bulnakov asked him where he was from, what he had studied, where he had worked, and why he had moved from Karlsruhe to Cucuron. "Ah, to be young! But I can understand—I didn't want to run my office in Paris anymore either, and moved here."

"Are you Russian?"

"I was born there, but grew up in Paris. We only spoke Russian at home, though. If the Russian market ever opens up to computers and software—I hope I'll live to see the day! By the way, here are two envelopes. One's for your work, the other for your expenses. It's an advance. Ah, here's Mademoiselle Kramsky."

She was wearing a summery dress with pale blue and red stripes and large blue flowers, a light blue belt, and a dark blue scarf. Her luxuriant, neatly combed hair hung to her shoulders, and again there was that friendliness in her eyes. She was amused at Monsieur Bulnakov fussing over them like a father seeing his two children off on a long trip, and hid her smile behind her hand. Georg noticed that her legs were short, and felt in a pleasant way that this brought her somewhat more down to earth. He was in love, but not yet aware of it.

They took the green Deux Chevaux. The car had been standing in the sun and was hot until they drove through the countryside with the top and windows open. There was a strong draft, and Georg stopped near Lourmarin, took a scarf out of his bag, and put it on. The radio was playing a mad potpourri of music: themes from Vivaldi to Wagner in a swinging pop sound, with an oily kitsch of lesser masterpieces in between. They made bets on what the next theme would be, and by the end she owed him three *petits blancs,* while he owed her five. They reached the hills before Bonnieux. The town on the hilltop shimmered in the midday sun, and they drove through its winding streets and past vineyards on their way down to the Route Nationale. They talked about music, movies, and where they lived, and over a picnic Georg told her about Heidelberg, Karlsruhe, and his life as a lawyer and with Hanne. He was surprised at how open he was. He felt strangely trusting and happy. As they drove on they dropped the formal *vous,* and she shook with laughter at how sharp and hard her name sounded in German.

"No, Françoise, it depends on how you pronounce it. The ending of your name can sound like an explosion or like a breath of air"—he demonstrated—"and . . . and . . . I would never call you Franziska in German."

"What would you call me?"

"Brown Eyes. You have the brownest eyes I've ever seen. You can't turn that into a name in French, but you can in German, and that's what I would call you."

She kept her eyes on the road. "Is that a term of endearment?"

"It's a term for someone one likes."

She looked at him earnestly. A lock of hair fell across her face. "I like driving with you through the countryside."

He turned onto the highway, stopped at a tollbooth, took a ticket, and threaded into the stream of cars.

"Will you tell me a story?" she asked.

He told her the tale of the little goose maid, speaking the rhymes first in German, then in French. He knew them by heart. When the false bride pronounced her verdict—"Naked as the day you were born you will be put in a barrel of sharp nails that two wild horses will drag till you die!"—Françoise caught her breath. She suspected what the old king would say: "False bride, you have just pronounced your own sentence! This will now be your own fate!"

As they drove toward Montélimar, she told him a Polish story in which a farmer outwits the devil. Then they sat listening in silence to Mozart's flute quartets on the radio. When Georg noticed that Françoise had fallen asleep he turned the music down, delighting in the motion of the car, the wind in his face, Françoise at his side, her breathing and contented sighs when her head tilted to one side and she sat up again, then rested her head on his shoulder.

In Lyon the hotels were all fully booked, and they had to drive six miles into the mountains and even there had to take a double room. Françoise's neck was sore, and Georg massaged it. They changed, drove into town, had a bite to eat, and then went to the mayor's reception, where they chatted with various people, their eyes often seeking each other out in the town hall. There was thick fog as they drove back to the hotel and Georg drove very slowly, keeping to the center line. "I like your sitting next to me," he said.

Then they lay next to each other in bed. Françoise told him about a lovesick friend of hers who had left for America only to fall unhappily in love there with a Lebanese man. As she reached over to the nightstand to turn out the light, Georg put his arm around her waist. She nestled against him in the dark. He caressed her, they kissed, and they could not get enough.

After they had made love, she cried quietly.

"What is it, Brown Eyes?"

She shook her head, and he kissed away the tears from her face.

6

THEY DIDN'T RETURN TO CADENET UNTIL Monday, though the conference was over on Friday. They went to St. Lattier, had dinner at the Lièvre Amoureux, and slept late on Saturday. They looked in their Michelin Guide for the restaurant Les Hospitaliers in Le Poët-Laval—it had a star—and they found a place to stay in the town. They spent their last night near Gordes, in the open. They didn't want their picnic to end: there was a mild evening breeze; the sky was full of stars, and in the coolness before dawn they slept cuddling beneath the blankets that Françoise kept in her car. It was a two-hour drive to Cadenet. The sun was shining, the air was clear, and the road was free. In the little towns through which they drove, stores were raising their shutters, cafés and bakeries were already open, and people were carrying home loaves of bread. Georg was at the wheel, Françoise's hand resting on his thigh. For a long time he was silent, and then he asked her, "Will you move in with me?"

He had been eagerly looking forward to his question and her response. He was certain she would say yes, that everything was perfect between the two of them. In fact—life was perfect.

The conference had been a success. He had come across as

relaxed and informed. Clever questions had been asked, and he had given witty answers. He had handed out not only Bulnakov's card but his own too, and a lawyer from Montélimar who specialized in computer leasing and software liability wanted to work with him on future French-German cases. The Xerox representative had been surprised when Georg told him about the TEXECT translation he had just done. "But that's been available in French for more than a year!" But what did Georg care, it wasn't his problem. In his jacket pocket he could feel Bulnakov's envelope with six thousand francs.

And Françoise was sitting beside him. The second night, Thursday, he had thrown all caution to the winds. He was going to enjoy it; he wasn't going to fall in love, wouldn't lose himself, but was still slightly afraid that this affair might last only one night, or a few days. He had woken up in the night and sat in the bathroom, his elbows propped on his knees, his head resting in his hands. He was moody and sad. Then Françoise came in, stood next to him, and he leaned his head against her bare hip while she ran her fingers through his hair. She said *Georg,* not *Georges* as she usually did. It sounded clumsy, but it made him feel good. He had told her that his parents and sister had called him Georg, his friends in high school and college too, but that when he went to France after his internship at the law firm it had become Georges or Shorsh. He had told her a lot about his childhood, his years at school and university, his marriage to Steffi, and the years with Hanne. She kept asking questions.

She didn't reveal much about herself—the silent type, he thought. It wasn't that she didn't talk. She described in great detail how she had moved from Paris to Cadenet, how she had found an apartment and fixed it up, how she settled in, what she did evenings and on weekends, and how she started making friends. She also answered his questions about Bulnakov's office in Paris, told him about the heart attack Bulnakov had had a year earlier, and his decision to work less and away from Paris. Bulnakov had wanted her to come with him, and had made her an offer she couldn't refuse. "You don't leave Paris for Cadenet just like that," she said. Her talk was mostly fast, lively, and amusing, and made Georg laugh a lot. "You're making fun of me," she'd say with a pout, and, hugging him, would give him a kiss.

They had arrived at Poët-Laval early, and after they carried their bags up to the room they couldn't get into bed fast enough. With one sweep he pulled his sweater, shirt, and T-shirt up over his head, with another his pants, underwear, and socks. They made love, fell asleep, and then, kissing and touching, were aroused again. She knelt on him, moving rhythmically, and stopped whenever his excitement grew too strong. Outside it was dusk, and her face and body shimmered in the twilight. He couldn't gaze at her enough, but had to close his eyes because he was brimming over with love and pleasure. She was next to him, and yet he still longed for her. "If you give me a child—you will be present when I give birth, won't you?" She looked at him intently. He nodded. Tears were running down his cheeks, and he couldn't speak.

They were approaching Bonnieux when he asked if she would move in with him. She stared straight ahead, and didn't say anything. She took her hand from his thigh and buried her face in her hands. He stopped the car at the top of the hill. Behind them lay the little town, and before them, in the shadow of the early morning, the ravine that cuts through the Luberon. He waited, not daring to ask any questions or to pull her hands from her face and see some terrible truth. Then she spoke, through her hands. He barely recognized her voice. It was colorless, timid, fending off, the voice of a little girl.

"I can't move in with you, Georg. Don't ask me why, don't press me—I can't. I would love to, it's so wonderful being with you, but

I can't, not yet. I can come to you, I can come to you often, and you can come to me. But please drop me off at my apartment now. I need to get ready quickly and go to the office. I'll call you."

"Why not come to the office with me right now? What about your car?" Georg asked, though he wanted to ask something quite different.

"I can't," she said, taking her hands from her face and wiping away her tears. "Drop me off at my place and then park the car somewhere near the office. I don't mind walking a little. You drive on."

"But Françoise, I don't understand. After the days we've just spent together."

She flung her arms around him. "They were wonderful, and I want more days like that. I want you to be happy." She kissed him. "Please, drive on now."

He drove on and dropped her off at her place. She had rented a former caretaker's lodge in a villa on the outskirts of the village. He wanted to take her bags in for her but she stopped him, insisting that he drive on. In his rearview mirror he saw her standing in front of the iron gate, between the stone posts crowned with stone globes and flanked on both sides by an old, thick box-tree hedge. She raised her hand and waved with a coquettish flutter of her fingers.

7

BULNAKOV HAD ASSUMED A SOMBER EXPRESSION. "Come in, my young friend. Sit down." He slumped heavily into the chair behind his desk and waved at the one across from him. A newspaper lay open in front of him. "You can fill me in about the IBM conference in the next day or so, there's no rush. But read this." He picked up a page from the newspaper and handed it to Georg. "I marked it with an *X*."

It was a short article: Last night Bernard M., the director of a Marseille translation agency, had had a fatal accident in his silver Mercedes on the Pertuis road. The police were still investigating the circumstances, and any witnesses were asked to contact the authorities.

"You worked for him, didn't you?" Bulnakov said, while Georg repeatedly read the short article.

"Yes, for almost two years."

"A great loss to our profession. You might think there's a dog-eat-dog war between our agencies, but the market isn't that small, and, I'm glad to say, respect and professional esteem are not impossible between competitors. I didn't know Maurin that long, but I had a high regard for him as a colleague. That's the first thing I wanted to say. The second thing, my young friend, is about the consequences his demise might have for you. You're good at what you do, you're young, you're going to make it in this world, but you've lost an important source of work. Well, there's always me, and I'm sure you can stand on your own two feet. But let me give you a bit of fatherly advice." Bulnakov smiled with a solicitous, friendly frown, and raised his hands in a gesture of blessing. He waited a moment, heightening the suspense, stretched it out even further, got up, walked to the other side of the desk, still without saying a word, his hands raised. Georg also stood up. He was looking at Bulnakov quizzically, inwardly amused. This must be what it was like asking a father for his daughter's hand. Bulnakov patted Georg on the shoulder. "Don't you agree?"

"I'm not sure yet what you're advising me to do."

"You see," Bulnakov said with a concerned look, "I'm aware of that, and it worries me. That young people nowadays find it hard to . . ."

"To do what?"

"Now, that's the right question!" Bulnakov said, exuding joy and benevolence once again. "To do what? To do what? Zeus asked that question, Lenin asked it, and there's only one answer: grab life by the horns. Seize the opportunities life presents you with, seize the opportunity offered you by Maurin's death. One man's demise is another man's prize. I know it's dreadful, but isn't it wonderful, too: the Wheel of Fortune? Talk to Maurin's widow, talk with your colleagues, take over his business!"

Of course Maurin's widow would be pleased if he took over the agency, paid her a percentage, and kept it running. Employees Chris, Isabelle, and Monique, Georg's colleagues working for Maurin, wouldn't be up to the task—a few weeks ago he wouldn't have been able to either—so they would surely continue working with him, for him.

"Thank you, Monsieur Bulnakov. You've given me very good advice. I suppose there's no time to lose. I ought to . . ."

"Indeed, there's no time to lose!" Bulnakov said, leading him to the door and patting him on the back.

The reception area was empty. Before Georg closed the door, Bulnakov called out after him to come back in two days for his next job.

Georg went out into the street and stopped in the square. Hadn't he left the car near the statue of the drummer boy? He looked up and down the square. He found it next to a construction site and got in, but then got out again and went into a bar on the corner. He took a cup of coffee and a glass of wine over to a table and stood beside it, looking out through the hazy window.

He felt weary with everything that lay ahead of him before he even started, before he could picture it. He drank the coffee, the wine, and ordered another glass. Then Nadine came in. She painted and made a living from pottery, making bowls, cups, plates—and producing homemade raisin bread. Thirty-six years old, interrupted studies, divorced, a ten-year-old son. She and Georg had slept together for a while on a whim, and then on a whim stopped sleeping together, though they kept on meeting with a burned-out familiarity.

"Maurin's dead. An accident. I've been weighing whether I ought to take over his business."

"Great idea!"

"A lot of work. I'm not sure that's what I want. But then again . . ." Georg ordered a third glass of wine and sat down next to Nadine. "Would you?"

"Take over Maurin's business? I thought writing was what you wanted to do. Didn't you tell me about some love story between a little boy and his teddy bear you were working on?"

"Yes, writing is what I want to do."

"And didn't you tell me that there was some American writer you wanted to translate and see published, and those mysteries by Solignac that nobody knows in Germany? But, that's the way things go: we always end up doing something other than what we want." She laughed a small, bitter laugh that was not without charm, brushed back a lock of hair from her face, and flicked the ash from her Gauloise. The scent of her perfume wafted over to Georg.

"Still wearing Opium?"

"Uh-huh. Did you know that of all the old crowd I'm the one who's been here longest? Some have left—I've no idea what they're up to—and others are either doing well or not so well. Some have gotten themselves jobs with the city or with the district administration, have a shop, or have hit the skids like Jacques, who's on drugs and has been doing some breaking and entering and will be caught one of these days. I like the fact that I'm somewhere in between, and I thought you'd hold out too."

"But you are painting. Don't tell me you don't want to have an exhibition someplace, or have people buy your paintings, or become famous."

"Sure I do. But I want my freedom, even if it doesn't amount to much. You're right, though—sometimes I do dream of exhibitions and all that, but I want to get to a point where I don't even dream about that kind of stuff anymore."

Georg drove home slightly tipsy, proud of his life, proud that he hadn't gone down the slippery slope or risen to the top through compromise. Nadine was right. But when he got home and saw the dirty dishes, and couldn't call Françoise because the phone had been cut off again since he hadn't paid the bill, he said to himself that enough was enough: "I'm fed up with this mess and with nothing going well for me, not having any money, wanting to write something but never getting anything written. My only

accomplishment in life is that I gave up a shaky law office in Karlsruhe for a shaky existence in Cucuron. I'll give Maurin's agency
a try!"

With this decision the weariness returned, and now also the fear
that he was taking on too much, that he would be out of his depth.
He lay down on the bed, fell asleep, and had nightmares about
agencies, unfinished jobs, unpaid bills, a ranting Bulnakov,
Françoise fending him off with frightened eyes, Maurin lying
dead. He woke up at four in the afternoon and was still worried.
He showered, put on a white shirt, a black tie, and his old gray
suit. By five-thirty he was in Marseille, ringing the doorbell of
Maurin's apartment.

8

"DO YOU REMEMBER WHEN WE WERE DRIVING from Gordes to Cadenet on Monday? I felt that the whole world lay at my feet. But then the feeling disappeared. I'm kind of fainthearted, and your not wanting to move in with me made me even more uncertain. But you were right: I wasn't yet the kind of man I wanted to be, the kind you could love."

Georg and Françoise were having an aperitif. The house was clean, the table set; a duck was roasting in the oven, oak logs burning in the fireplace; clean sheets were on the bed.

"Here's to us," he said.

Their glasses met. She was wearing a red dress with a zipper down its whole length, a prim, girlish pin in her hair, and her perfume—"You look wonderfully enticing."

She laughed and held out her hand across the table for him to kiss. "The dress is old, I didn't have time to wash my hair, and as for Jil Sander, I'd say her Eau de Toilette is austere rather than seductive. Why don't you fill me in on everything that happened this week. I was waiting for you to call or come by. I thought you'd at least come to the office to pick up some work. And then Bulnakov tells me you're inviting me to dinner on Saturday, all the while dropping hints that when I saw you I wouldn't recognize you. That wasn't fair," she added with a pout, "even if the invitation was very sweet. I don't see why I shouldn't have recognized you. You're even wearing the same jeans you had on last weekend."

Georg got up. "Allow me to introduce myself, Mademoiselle. Georg Polger, director, president, and CEO of Marseille's famous Maurin Translation Service, the most successful translation agency from Avignon to Cannes, and from Grenoble to Corsica!" He bowed.

"What? What do you mean?"

Georg told her what had happened. He described Madame Maurin, with her excessively blond hair, heavy makeup, her excessively tight skirt, and her exaggerated mourning. The only genuine things about her were her hard eyes and even harder sense of business. It was good that he had come; she'd already been made various offers, but, needless to say, former employees would be given preference. Then she named an absurdly high price. Georg had remained cool and polite. That same evening he had called on Chris, Isabelle, and Monique to make sure they would stay with the firm. He spent the night in Marseille and set up an appointment with Industries Aéronautiques Mermoz in Toulon for Tuesday morning. "That was the hardest nut to crack," he told Françoise. "A young manager, dark blue suit and vest, gold-rimmed glasses, cold as ice. Luckily he foresaw a lot of translation work over the next few months and had intended to hire Maurin's agency, but hadn't heard about the fatal car crash. And luckily the manager was up on the technical details of the helicopter they were working on, and I threw some terminology at him that I picked up from my jobs last year, until he got the point he needed a professional for the translations and I was that professional. I proposed the same terms Maurin had always had with them, and naturally gave him the line about all this being on a trial basis and so on. But from what I gathered, all they want is for the translations to be reliable and on time. And that they will be."

"What about Madame Maurin?"

"Do you remember Maxim, the lawyer from Montélimar we met at the conference in Lyon? I gave him a call and asked him about the legal details of taking over an agency of this kind. Then, when I went back to Madam Maurin and flung my trump card on the table, that I was already working with Mermoz, she saw reason. She'll be getting 12 percent of our turnover over a five-year period. She and I sifted through her husband's correspondence, and notified all our clients about the takeover. The funeral was Thursday— I was standing at the widow's side, and on Friday Maxim came over to set up the contract, by which time we'd already gotten our first jobs from Mermoz. So this morning I finally got back from Marseille to Cucuron."

"At the funeral you were at Madame Maurin's side? When's the happy day?"

"Don't be silly!" Georg said. He looked at Françoise. Was she jealous? Was she poking fun at him?

"Oh no, the duck!"

He ran into the kitchen and poured gravy over the hissing brown meat.

Françoise sat at the table, fiddling with her knife and fork. "Will you be moving to Marseille?" she asked. "I . . . I have . . . oh, come here, my fainthearted lover."

She pulled him down onto her knee, wrapped her arms around his stomach, and lay her head on his chest. She looked up at him. "I've been thinking about you and me."

Again he saw the dimple by her eyebrow. "I see you're still thinking."

"Stop it. You're making fun of me. I'm being serious. You asked if I'd move in with you. I felt you were going too fast, that I need time. But when I didn't see you all week, when I couldn't touch you, feel you, I thought . . . You know what I'm trying to say, and you're just sitting there like a tin soldier!"

He went on sitting there like a tin soldier, saying nothing and gazing at her happily.

"If you're not moving to Marseille, and have a glass for my toothbrush," she said, "if you can make some space in your closet and give me a desk and a shelf, then—I don't want to give up my apartment, but I'd like to spend a lot of time here with you. Is that okay?"

9

GEORG COULDN'T REMEMBER EVER BEING as happy as he was the next few months.

Françoise moved in at the end of March. Spring exploded into a luxuriant summer. The year before the garden hadn't blossomed with so much color, the days had not been as bright, the nights not as mild. When the heat began in June and the earth grew dry, Georg saw a gentle radiance instead of parched dryness. And he saw Françoise growing more and more beautiful. Her skin became tanned, delicate, and smooth. She gained weight, grew more curvaceous and feminine, which he liked.

There were times when the work and all the commuting between Marseille and Cucuron were too much, but four times a week he managed to be at the office by nine, to assign work to Chris, Monique, and Isabelle, edit their translations, and do some translating himself. He managed to make deadlines, keep old clients and bring in new ones, and install a word-processing system. In April an officer from National Security asked him questions about his citizenship, work, lifestyle, and political views. He asked Georg for references in Germany, and had him sign a consent form that would allow National Security to request information from the German authorities. In May Georg received a confirmation from Mermoz that he had been given security clearance, and that all confidential materials sent to his agency would have to be translated by him personally. Now the work really began. There was hardly a weekend when he didn't have to spend hours poring over construction plans, manuals, lists of materials, and flowcharts. He managed that too.

As a boy he had never had an electric train. His father had given him a heavy, metallic locomotive that could be wound up, two railway cars, and a few tracks, enough to form a circle. At Christmas Georg had gazed longingly at the store window of Knoblauch's, the biggest toy store in Heidelberg, where toy trains rolled over an extensive network of tracks—lots of trains at once, with no collisions or derailments, with blinking signals and barriers being raised and lowered. He was able to see a shop assistant maneuvering the trains from a small podium.

That was how Georg felt now. In fact, it *was* too much. Just as the store window hadn't been big enough for all the trains, his resources were too limited for all the work he was getting. There ought to have been constant collisions and mishaps, but it could all be managed if one concentrated. Like trains, the jobs could be coupled and uncoupled, maneuvered past one another, put on standby, accelerated, or brought to a stop. He was in complete command, and applied his concentration with gusto.

Françoise was usually at home when he came back from work in the evening. She was watching for him, came to the door when she heard his car, and ran to meet him, throwing her arms around him. Sometimes, as they ran the few steps to the house, she pulled off his jacket and tie, which he now almost always wore, and led him straight into the bedroom. Georg pretended to be aloof, and let her seduce him. Sometimes she greeted him with a stream of words, telling him about her workday, Bulnakov, or Claude, a nearby farmer who came by from time to time in his Citroën van to pick up stale bread for his geese, and to drop off cabbages, watermelons, and tomatoes. Sometimes she had already cooked dinner, other times they cooked together. In the morning Georg always got up first, did the dishes from the night before, made tea, and took it to Françoise, who was still in bed. He loved waking her up. He slipped back under the covers, felt her warm body, and tasted the familiarity of her sleepy breath. In the morning her light girlish voice was hidden beneath a smoky hoarseness. It aroused him, but she didn't want to make love in the morning.

The appearance of the rooms changed. Françoise fixed up the one at the end of the upstairs hall for herself. She sewed a cover for the frayed armchair by the fireplace; in the bedroom, curtains for the alcove, where there was a chaos of jackets, pants, shirts, and underwear. In the kitchen a trash can replaced the plastic bags, and a small cabinet was installed in the bathroom for the toiletries that had been scattered all over the place. Françoise bought the tablecloths in Aix.

"Where did you learn to do all this?" Georg asked her.

"What do you mean?"

"Well, cooking, sewing, and"—he was standing in the dining room, a Pernod in his hand, indicating in a wide arc the whole house—"and all this magic?"

After he had broken up with Hanne, he had often had the urge to move out. Now he once again liked where and how he was living.

"We women have a flair for this sort of thing," Françoise replied, with a coquettish smile.

"No, I'm serious. Did your mother teach you how to do all this?"

"You're such a nosy, fretful boy. It's a knack I have—isn't that all that matters?"

One evening in June, Georg didn't come back from Marseille until very late. He stopped on the hill, from which the house was already visible. The garden gate stood open, the windows of the kitchen, the dining room, and living room were lit, as was the light on the terrace. Music wafted gently toward him. Françoise liked turning up the stereo.

Georg sat in the car and gazed at the house. It was a warm night, and the anticipation of coming home surged warmly within him: In a few minutes, he thought, I will be outside the house, the door will open, she will come out, and we will embrace. Then we will have a Campari with grapefruit juice and dinner, and we'll talk and make out. Françoise was on edge and sensitive these days, and he had to be especially loving and gentle. He looked forward to that too.

As they lay in bed, he asked her if she wanted to marry him. She tensed up in his arms and remained silent.

"Hey, Brown Eyes. What's wrong?"

She freed herself from his embrace, turned on the light, and sat up. She looked at him in despair. "Why can't you let things be just the way they are? Why do you always have to crowd me, push me into a corner?"

"But what did I . . . I love you, I've never loved anyone like this, and everything is so great, and never . . ."

"Then why change anything, why? I'm sorry, darling. You're wonderful. I don't want to upset you. I just want you to be happy."

She nestled up to him, kissing him again and again. At first he wanted to withdraw, push her away, and talk things through. But when he held her away from him at arm's length and looked into her blank, distant face, he gave up. He let her kiss and bite his nipples, and do all the things she knew aroused him. His orgasm came, she held him tight, and then, in the numbness of approaching sleep, he felt that his proposal had become unreal.

IO

HER REACTION WHEN HE PROPOSED TO HER was not the only warning. Later he saw all the signals for what they had been, and realized that he hadn't wanted to see them.

Her sudden departures. He would come home Friday evening from Marseille, and Françoise would be waiting for him in a wonderful weekend mood. They'd go to dine at Les Vieux Temps, and would talk all evening with Gérard and Catrine, and then Saturday fritter away the morning. In the afternoon he had to translate. He would finish his quota by Saturday evening or Sunday morning, and they would have breakfast, stroll through the vineyards, or by the tomato and melon fields, or through the woods on the slopes of the Luberon. When they returned they would lie down, and have a cup of tea or glass of champagne in bed. That was how their typical weekend passed. And Françoise's leaving suddenly at four or five in the afternoon on Sundays had almost become a part of the weekend routine.

"I have to go now."

"You do?" Georg asked the first time, taken aback. He tried to hold on to her, to pull her back. She wriggled free, and he got up to dress. She sat down on the edge of the bed, already wearing her skirt and blouse.

"You don't have to get up, darling," she said. "Stay in bed and get some rest." She tucked him in and kissed him. "I just need some time to myself. I'm going to head home and take care of a few things, and call Mom and Dad. Tomorrow evening, when you get back from Marseille, I'll be waiting for you."

Georg would perhaps have come to terms with this had Françoise kept only Sunday evenings for herself. But she said she needed some time to herself, then that she had to take care of important business for Bulnakov, or that she was expecting an important phone call she simply had to take at home. This didn't happen often during the week. But there were times when she suddenly got up and left after dinner, or after he'd fallen asleep. He kept trying to stop her from leaving—with questions, or a sharp or ironic word or two—but always came up against her unyielding resistance. She warded him off tenderly, angrily, or desperately, but in the end she always left. The first few times, he did remain in bed. But it was usually dusk when she left, and he found the aching beauty of the twilight hour alone painful, with her scent in his bed. So he too would dress, go with her downstairs, and stand at the garden gate until he could no longer see her car.

One weekend he had picked her up at Bulnakov's office on Friday afternoon, and so she had to ask him to drive her home on Sunday when she needed to go. He took advantage of the situation, kept stalling and saying "Just a second," and they made love one more time. She wanted to get it over with quickly, but he kept her at it, and it was so wonderful for her that she could not leave. Finally she begged him to make her come. Not because she was anxious to leave, but because she couldn't stand it anymore. And when he did, she was ecstatic. As he drove her home she nestled up against him and whispered tenderly, all the while urging him to drive faster. "Oh God, I'm going to be late! What did I want that orgasm for?"

She rarely invited him into her apartment, two adjoining rooms on the ground floor, a bathroom, a kitchen, and a terrace outside the larger room. The place felt unlived-in. He took a few snapshots of her, though she didn't like being photographed: Françoise on the terrace, Françoise hanging out the washing, Françoise standing in front of the refrigerator, or sitting on the couch beneath a large drawing of a church facade that had been executed with architectural precision.

"What's the church?" he asked.

She hesitated. "That's the cathedral in Warsaw in which my parents got married."

He knew she had parents, but knew nothing about them. "When did they leave Poland?"

"I didn't say they weren't still living in Warsaw."

"But you often talk to them on the phone," he said, unable to make sense of it.

The washing machine stopped and Françoise went to unload it. He followed her.

"Why are you so secretive about your parents?"

"Why do you want to know so much about my family? You've got me—isn't that enough?"

In July Georg had a party. He had long dreamed of inviting everyone he knew and liked: his parents, sister, uncles and aunts, business associates, colleagues and friends—old friends from Germany and new ones he had met in Provence.

The party would begin in the afternoon, they would have fun, dance, and it would all end with a big fireworks display. His relatives couldn't come and only a few of his German friends showed up, but the party was fun, and the last guests left at dawn. Initially

Georg had wanted to surprise Françoise, but then he decided that her friends and relatives should come too. She did write a few invitations and help him with the preparations, but when she drove over to Marseille on the morning before the party to get some fresh oysters, she called to say that she wouldn't be able to make it because she had to fly to Paris on business. Nor did anyone she had invited show up.

On the afternoon after the party, Georg was sitting on the terrace drinking champagne with some old friends from Heidelberg. They had gone for a long hike while the cleaning ladies from the office had removed the last traces of the party. His friends had to head back to Germany, but they kept on talking and putting off their departure. The familiarity of long friendship was like the warm bed one doesn't want to leave in the morning.

Françoise came driving down the hill in her green Deux Chevaux. Georg jumped up, opened the garden gate, and opened the car door for her. She got out, saw his friends, greeted them awkwardly, and hurried into the kitchen to put away some things she had brought, staying there quite a while. Then she came out and joined the others, but didn't fit in. Gerd asked her about her flight to Paris, but she avoided the question. Walter asked when she and Georg were planning to marry, at which she blushed bright red. Jan said that he heard she was from Poland and that he'd just been to Warsaw, and began talking about his trip, but she didn't say anything. Gerd made a few pleasant remarks about the difficulties that a new girlfriend encountered with her boyfriend's old friends, but she didn't seem to be listening. After half an hour the friends from Heidelberg left, and while Georg was still standing next to Françoise at the door waving, she hissed at him, "What did you tell them about me?"

"Why are you in such a bad mood, Brown Eyes? What's wrong?"

But she was in a bad mood and shouted at him in a little girl's voice, fretful and cantankerous, her sentences starting with "And let me tell you!" "And if you think!" and "Of one thing you can be certain!" He didn't know what to say, and stood there flustered.

That evening she said she was sorry, boiled the asparagus she had brought, and pressed herself into his arms. "I had the impression you were talking about me, and that your friends had already come to conclusions about me, and wouldn't see the real me anymore. I'm sorry. I ruined your afternoon."

Georg was understanding. The trip to Paris must have been stressful. In bed she said, "Georges, why don't we go visit your friends in Heidelberg some weekend. I'd like to get to know them better. They seem really nice." Georg fell asleep happy.

II

IT WAS THE END OF JULY. Georg woke up in the night in the dark room, rolled sleepily onto his stomach, and tried to lay one of his legs across Françoise. Her side of the bed was empty.

He waited for the sound of the flushing toilet and her footsteps on the stairs. Did minutes pass, or had he fallen asleep and woken up again? He still didn't hear anything. Where was she? Wasn't she feeling well?

He got up, put on a bathrobe, and went out into the hall. A thin strip of light was shining along the floor from under the door to his study. He opened the door. "Françoise!"

It took him a few seconds to grasp the situation. Françoise, sitting at his desk, turned and looked at him. Like a gazelle, he thought. A hurt, startled gazelle. He noticed her aquiline nose, and her frightened eyes fending him off; her mouth opened slightly, tensely, as if she were sucking in air. The plans that Georg was translating lay on the desk, held in place on either side by books, and illuminated by his table lamp. Françoise was naked, the blanket with which she had wrapped herself had slipped off. "What in heaven's name are you doing?" A stupid question. What was she doing with a camera and his plans? She put the camera on the table and covered her breasts with her hands. She was still looking at him distraught, without saying anything. He noticed the dimple over her right eyebrow.

He laughed. As if he could laugh the situation away, as he had during fights with Hanne and Steffi, when he had escaped, incredulous and helpless, into a foolish laugh. The situation was so absurd. This sort of thing never happened. Not to him, Georg. But his laughter didn't wipe away the situation. He felt tired, his head empty. His mouth hurt from laughing. "Come back to bed."

"I haven't finished yet," she said, looking at the plans and reaching for her camera.

"Who are you?" The situation was still absurd, and Françoise's naked breasts struck him as obscene. Her voice had again the shrill rasp of a distraught little girl. He tore the camera out of her hand and threw it against the wall, seized the desk, and shoved its top off its trestle. The lamp fell on the floor and went out. He wanted to shake her, hit her. But as the light went out, his anger went out too. It was dark, he took a step forward, tripped, pushed over a filing cabinet, fell, and hit his leg. He heard Françoise crying. He reached out for her and tried to embrace her. She flailed and kicked, sobbed and whimpered, and grew wilder, until she collided with the chair and fell crashing against the bookshelf.

Suddenly it was quiet. He got up and turned on the light. She was lying curled up by the shelf, motionless. "Françoise!" He crouched down at her side, felt for a wound on her head, found nothing, picked her up, and carried her to bed. When he came with a bowl and a towel she looked at him with a faint smile. He sat down by the bed.

Still the voice of a little girl, now begging, imploring: "I am sorry, I didn't want to hurt you, I didn't want to do this. It's got nothing to do with you. I love you, I love you so much. You mustn't be angry with me, it's not my fault. They forced me to do it, they . . ."

"Who are they?"

"You must promise me you won't do anything foolish. What do we care about those helicopters and . . ."

"Jesus! I want to know what this is all about!"

"I'm frightened, Georges." She sat up and huddled against him. "Hold me, hold me tight."

Finally she told him. He gradually understood that what she was telling him was really their story, with the two of them, the real Françoise and the real Georg, that it was part of their lives like his house and his car, his office in Marseille, his jobs and projects, his love for Françoise, his getting up in the morning, his going to bed at night.

She assumed they had already targeted him when they sent Bulnakov and her to Pertuis. Who were "they"?

"The Polish secret service, and behind them the KGB—don't ask me, I don't know. They arrested my brother and father, right when martial law was declared. I've been working for them ever since. They released my father, but they told me they'd come get him again if I didn't continue. . . . As for my brother . . ." She sobbed, covering her face with her hands. "They told me his life depends on me. His death warrant has been signed, and whether he will be pardoned depends on . . . He had called for open resistance and thrown a Molotov cocktail when the militia cleared the square in front of the university—as far as I know the only Molotov cocktail thrown in all of Poland at that time—and the driver and the passenger were burned in the car. He has . . . he is . . . I love my brother very much, Georges. Ever since Mother died, he was the most important person in my life, until . . ." She sobbed. "Until I met you."

"And you're ready to have me thrown in jail in order to get your brother out?"

"But everything's going so well. You're happy, and so am I.

What do we care about these helicopters? Soon my people will have what they want, my brother will get his pardon, and they'll leave us alone, and then . . . You asked me if I will live with you. I want to so much, I can't live without you anymore, I want to be with you always, it's only that . . . Don't you see why I couldn't just say yes back then? Please, please . . ."

Again the voice and look of a little girl, frightened because she'd done something bad, hopeful because she'd made up for it all, and sulking, because he hadn't rewarded her for it yet.

"Why would they leave you alone once they have the documents they want?"

"They promised. They said they'd release my father, and they kept their promise."

"You'd never have worked for them if they hadn't let him go. They'll commute your brother's death sentence to life in prison, at which point you'll go on working for them so they will reduce his sentence to fifteen years, and they can keep on haggling further reductions. You won't have a choice."

She didn't say anything, but continued to look at him, sulking. "It goes without saying that they have to offer you something so you will keep up the work," he continued. "Let's say three years off his sentence for every year that you work for them. That means they have you where they want you for at least another five years. You're good at what you do, you're fluent in French, know the country and the people. Believe me, they'll keep you where they want you. How long were you already in France when they recruited or forced you into this?"

"It sounds like you're cross-examining me! I don't like talking with you like this."

He had moved to the edge of the bed, his back straight, his hands cradling his stomach. He was staring intently. "It's not only you they have—they've got me too. And when they're done with the attack helicopter, they'll set their sights on the stealth reconnaissance plane, or the new control system or bomb, or God knows what! Once I've worked for them for a long time, they've got me where they want me, even without you. Is this what you wanted? Is this how you want us to live?"

"Our life isn't all that bad. We've got each other, a nice house, enough money. And nobody need know that you're aware of what's going on. Why can't things just go on the way they are? Weren't you happy all this time?"

He said nothing. He looked out the window into the night and felt heavy with fatigue. What she was saying was true, but then again, it also wasn't. What did he care about helicopters, fighter jets, reconnaissance planes, bombers, and all the maneuverings surrounding the arms race, armament, and disarmament? Since he didn't have the time or money to write a novel, he didn't care what he was translating or for whom: IBM, Mermoz—why not for the Poles and Russians too? It wouldn't involve any more work; he laughed bitterly. But his freedom was done for. He felt this with painful clarity. He was no longer sitting on the podium maneuvering all the trains, but was a train himself that others could set in motion, bring to a halt, start up again, accelerate, and stop.

"Georg?"

He shrugged his shoulders despondently. Had his early freedom been just an illusion? He remembered her sudden departures on Sundays.

"Why did you always have to deliver the negatives of the plans on Sunday?" he asked her.

"What?"

He didn't repeat the question. Something didn't fit. Just didn't fit. Something kept buzzing in his mind, not a clear thought, but perhaps just the disbelief that all this should have happened to him, and that the way he was living would go on, but look very different from this point.

She sighed and laid her head in his lap. Her left hand caressed his back, and her right hand slid beneath his bathrobe, reaching gently between his legs. Surprised, and as if from a distance, he felt his arousal.

"Are you . . . were you Bulnakov's lover?"

She let go and sat up. "What kind of a question is that? How mean and spiteful! I haven't been with anyone else since I met you, and as for what happened in the past, it doesn't concern either of us. Not to mention that if Bulnakov had wanted to sleep with me, I would hardly have had a choice."

"What about now?"

"I have no choice now either, if you want to know!" she shouted. "I let him do his thing, then he gets up, buttons his pants, and tucks in his shirt. Shall I show you? Go on, lie down, you be me and I'll be him, go on!" She tried to pull Georg onto the bed, tugged at him, her hands striking out. Then she began to sob, and she curled up like a fetus.

Georg sat there, his hand on her shoulder. Finally he lay down next to her. They made love. Outside, the sun was rising and the first birds were beginning to sing.

12

SHE GOT UP AT DAYLIGHT. He stayed in bed, listening to her movements in the next room, the flushing toilet, the clattering dishes in the kitchen, the sound of the shower. She opened the living-room shutters, which banged loudly against the outside wall, and he waited for her car to start. But she must have sat down in the rocking chair with a cup of coffee. It was a while before the hinges of the outer gate creaked and the engine of her Deux Chevaux started up with a stutter and the gravel rasped under the tires. Wrapped in the scent of their body and their love, exhausted by the nocturnal battle, he listened to the car drive away.

He woke up again hours later. The sun was shining into the room. He didn't have the strength to get up; he barely wanted to move into a more comfortable position. Then he did get up, without knowing why, or why exactly at that moment. He got up. He showered, dressed, made coffee, drank it, fed the cats. He did this all with a strange lightness. He looked for money in the drawer and found it, put on his jacket, took the keys, locked the door, got into his car, and drove off. His movements were controlled. He monitored the road before him closely, the potholes, the cars turning out from side roads, the cars coming toward him. He drove fast, carefully, detached. He felt as if he wasn't driving, as if he could plow into a tractor or a tree without getting hurt, without so much as denting his car. He parked under the plane trees by the pond and went into the pharmacy. Here too he felt as if he were watching himself from a distance. As he walked, his movements were light. It was as if only the shell of his body were walking, as if he were empty inside and the shell was porous, letting in light and air.

In the pharmacy he stood a few minutes in line, waiting his turn. When he entered he had said "bonjour" without putting on a friendly, happy face, and as he stood and waited, his face showed neither expectation nor impatience—nor any interest in Madame Revol's small talk with the other customers. He felt that his face was like an empty page.

"Could I please have a box of Dovestan?"

"Monsieur would do better to have a beer or a glass of red wine before going to bed. Dovestan is a dangerous drug. I read that in Germany or Italy you can't even get it without a prescription anymore."

He hadn't intended to reply, but Madame Revol was showing no sign of going to the medicine shelf. She looked at him with a worried, motherly expression, waiting for him to say something. He put on a playful smile. "And that's exactly why I live in France, Madame," he said, laughing. "But jokes aside, I don't seem to get any sleep when there's a full moon. And I'd hate to think what would happen to my liver with all the red wine I'd have to gulp down."

The instant Madame Revol gave him the pills he knew he wouldn't take them. Suicide? No, not him. Those Russians, Poles, Bulnakov, Françoise—they had another thing coming! Wasn't he holding all the cards? Wasn't it up to him to deliver or not to deliver, to go to the police or not, to string Bulnakov along, and make him pay?

He drank a glass of white wine in the Bar de l'Étang and then another. Back at home he went into his study. The desk was standing upright again, the plans laid out, the camera gone. Françoise had clearly finished taking pictures that morning. Georg put in a call to his office in Marseille. His secretary had been expecting him, but had managed things on her own, rescheduling appointments and appeasing clients. Then he dialed Bulnakov's number.

"Hello?"

"Hello, Polger speaking. We need to talk. I'd like to drop by at four."

"Drop by, my young friend, drop by! Though I must say you're sounding a little secretive. What's all this about?"

So Françoise hadn't told him anything. Was she going to tell him, or didn't she intend to?

"We can talk about that later. Till then, Monsieur." Georg hung up. He had to go for it, use the element of surprise, confuse his opponent—he would make Bulnakov sweat.

And, in fact, when Georg turned up at four Bulnakov did have large sweaty patches under his arms. The doors were open, Françoise was not at her desk, and Bulnakov was sitting regally in his office, his jacket draped over the back of his chair, the top buttons of his shirt and pants undone. *Then he gets up, buttons his pants, and tucks in his shirt,* shot through Georg's mind.

"Come in, my young friend. I'm trying to get some fresh air in here, but I can't get a draft going and lose heat." He heaved himself up out of the chair, buttoned his pants, and tucked in his shirt. Georg was jealous, hurt, furious. He didn't shake Bulnakov's hand.

"The game is over, Monsieur," Georg said, sitting down on the edge of the table by the sofas. He towered over Bulnakov, who had sat down again at his desk.

"What game are you talking about?"

"Whatever it is, I'm no longer playing along. It's up to you whether I go to the police or not. If I'm not to go, then Françoise's brother must be pardoned and given authorization to leave Poland. You have three days."

Bulnakov gave Georg a friendly look. Laugh lines crinkled the corners of his eyes, his mouth widened, his plump cheeks shone. He squeezed the tip of his nose, lost in thought. "Is this the same boy who stood before me in this office only a few months ago? No, it isn't. You have become a man, my young friend. I like you. From what I see, the thing you are calling my 'game' has done you quite a bit of good. But now you want out." He shook his head, puffed up his cheeks, and blew the air out between his lips. "No, my young friend. Our train is on a roll, it's rolling at great speed, and you can't get off. If you try to jump, you'll end up with broken bones. But a train moving fast also gets where it's going quickly. Just be a little patient."

"Why should I?"

"What is it you want to tell the police?"

The conversation wasn't going the way Georg had imagined. He felt he was losing the upper hand. "Leave that up to me," he said. "You might think I don't have proof. But perhaps I do. And then again I might only have my story and a few scraps of evidence. But once the police know where to look and what to look for, they'll find the rest too. I've seen the efficiency of the Polish secret service—now you'll see how efficient the French are."

"How prettily you craft your sentences. We might let the French police find this or that roll of film with your fingerprints on it. And you can be sure we will let them find the fender of your yellow Peugeot—the one that forced Maurin's Mercedes off the road—not to mention that we'll point the police in the direction of the garage in Grenoble that repaired the damage to your car." Bulnakov's tone was still friendly. "Why make yourself and Françoise unhappy? A few more weeks and it'll all be over. We'll part as good friends—or good enemies—either way, we'll part amicably. Things will work out for her brother too—he's quite obstinate, that one, not to mention thick-skulled. And if you and Françoise want to marry: why not? You're the right age."

Georg sat there stunned. There was a sound of footsteps. He turned and saw Françoise standing in the doorway.

"Is it true, Françoise, that my fingerprints are on the negatives?" She looked from Georg to Bulnakov and back.

"I had to do it that way. You take so many pictures—I used your film cans." She bit her lip.

"We were in Lyon when Maurin . . . when he was murdered. I'm sure the people at the conference and the hotel receptionist will remember me."

"Tell him, Françoise."

She hung her head. "The night when Maurin . . . That night we weren't in Lyon anymore. We weren't in the hotel either. We were out in that meadow near Gordes."

"But you can back me up . . ." Georg didn't finish the sentence. He was beginning to understand. Bulnakov was frowning, yet was looking at Georg not with irritation, but with pity. Françoise's face was cold and unapproachable. "This can't be, Brown Eyes. I can't believe you did all this on purpose." He was saying it more to himself than to her. Then he jumped up, seized her, and shook her. "Tell me it isn't true! Tell me it isn't! Tell me!" As if his shaking and shouting would break the armor that encased Françoise, Françoise whom he had held in his arms, who had opened up to him, to whom he had opened up, the real Françoise.

"Why did you have to ruin everything?" she said. "Why couldn't you just leave things the way they were?" She didn't try to defend herself, but kept complaining in her thin, shrill child's voice and remained unapproachable. Only when he let her go, she shouted: "I won't take this from you, Georg! I won't! I never promised you anything! I never played games! I was me, and you were you! You were the one who wouldn't listen and wouldn't face reality! It was you who got your hopes up! And now you see that there was nothing there! Don't think I don't know what you're playing at: you've ruined everything so you can get back at me! You were miserable because you couldn't have me, and so you want to go to the police so I'll be miserable too. Don't think for a moment that I'm going to side with you or back you up. If you go to the police, you've lost me!" She was shaking.

"What reality wouldn't I face?" Georg asked. He was grimacing like a madman, but making a last-ditch effort.

"So go to the police! Go ahead, ruin everything we had together! You're such a weakling, such a coward! Instead of finishing what you started, instead of seeing it through, you have to destroy everything. Well, go to the police! But don't you think . . ." Her voice hissed, her words were crystal clear, her sentences a farce of logical reasoning. He heard the spite in her voice, and lost control of the situation, like a man whose expensive watch falls into deep waters, and who, even as it is falling, before it plunges into the water and disappears, realizes its final loss. Perhaps it could still be caught, by a fast snatch or a leap, but he feels a lameness that turns into the numbness of the pain of loss.

He shrugged his shoulders. Feeling empty, he walked past Françoise and out of the office.

"Wait a moment, my young friend, wait. . . ." Bulnakov called out after him, but Georg didn't turn around.

13

HE WALKED PAST THE STATUE OF THE DRUMMER BOY and went into the bar on the corner. LE TAMBOUR D'ARCOLE—it was the first time he'd read the statue's inscription. He tried to remember what heroic role the drummer boy had played in the Battle of Arcole. Thinking of heroism made him wince, and he ordered coffee and wine. This time the window was clean, and the town square lay clearly before him under the blue sky of the afternoon.

What was so bad? His attempt to threaten them with the police in order to save Françoise's brother had misfired. But damn the whole Kramsky clan. All the translations he'd done had ended up with the Polish or Soviet secret service. But the games the big powers played with soldiers, cannons, tanks, planes, and helicopters would go on. Georg imagined generals standing in a sandbox, one going *"b-r-r-r-r"* with a toy helicopter in his hand, the other *"s-h-h-h-h"* with an airplane. Had they really killed Maurin in order to give him, Georg, access to the Mermoz plans? He and Françoise had indeed driven to the conference in Lyon in her Citroën. He'd left his Peugeot in Cadenet, and when they got back from Lyon he hadn't found it where he thought he'd parked it. He felt a surge of fear. He steadied his nerves: would they really risk everything by letting him go to the police?

And what about Françoise? He felt it was all over between the two of them, but he didn't love her any less, or feel any less close to her than—than yesterday. A day ago his world had still been intact.

He felt as if he were sitting in a hospital bed after an amputation, looking for the first time at a leg that was no longer there and over which the sheet no longer bulged. The eye sees it, the mind registers it, and yet the patient expects that ultimately he will get up and walk away, with his toe itching.

Georg looked out the window. Françoise was coming out of a side street onto the square. She walked toward her car, stopped, walked a few steps farther, and stopped again. She had seen his parked car. Slowly she turned and looked in the direction of the bar where he was sitting. Dazzled by the sun she craned her neck, trying to catch sight of him. Then she walked toward the bar. He saw her bouncy tread, and her fast steps echoed in his ear, though he couldn't hear them. She was wearing a black outfit and had a bright sweater draped over her shoulders, its sleeves tied above her chest.

His heart had always skipped a beat when he saw her coming from a distance, lost in thought, stopping by a storefront or a street musician and then strolling on and, upon catching sight of him, coming toward him with a quick step, a fluttering wave of her hand, and an expectant smile. Why did you betray me, he thought, why. . . .

"I've got to rush—see you this evening?" she called out, popping her head in at the door. Then she was outside again. She sounded as she always did. He watched her hurry off, and finished his wine. On the way home he did some shopping, for both of them, as always. When she came home, roulades were simmering in the pot, a fire was burning in the fireplace, and music was playing. Amazed, he had seen himself going through the motions of shopping, tidying up, cooking. This isn't really happening, it's not real, this isn't me. But he had managed to do everything with great ease.

Neither of them touched on the subject of the night before or the afternoon in Bulnakov's office. They trod carefully, hesitantly, and he was taken aback at feeling the excitement of their first meeting. Later, in bed, after they had made love, he turned the light back on, sat up, and looked at her. "What is to become of us?" he asked.

She looked at him calmly. Georg couldn't tell if the dimple over her right eyebrow indicated that she was thinking, or that she simply didn't know what to say. Then she picked up the little crocheted bear by the radio alarm on Georg's side, sat the bear on her chest, and brought its paws together in a begging motion.

"I want you to be happy," she said. "Really happy."

Nothing he would say could reach her. All he could do was throw her out, but he didn't have the strength.

The next morning he drove to Marseille, gave the messenger from Mermoz the translated plans, and was given new ones. He wondered whether he should do the translation at home or at the office. He decided to make photocopies, even though the security regulations forbade it. He locked the originals away and took the copies home.

Around ten in the evening he heard her Citroën. He folded the copies, waited until she entered the house, and then went out onto the balcony by his study, where he hid the papers in a drainpipe. When she came in, she found him at his desk writing a letter. The same thing happened the following evening, and the one after that. Then she asked him at breakfast quite casually, while busying herself with her coffee, croissant, and eggs, "Hasn't Mermoz been giving you any work these days?"

"I can't complain."

She stirred her coffee, though she hadn't put either milk or sugar in it. "Don't do anything silly, Georg." Her voice sounded soft.

He was relieved when he had finished transcribing his translation from the copy onto the original plan and handed it in. Then he sat a long time studying the copies and the new plans, understanding more and more what he was dealing with. It had something to do with suspensions, which had been clear enough during the translation work. But what was supposed to be suspended, and where? Again he locked away the originals and put a copy in his briefcase.

As he drove home he sang at the top of his voice, feeling that he had won, that he had escaped the net in which Bulnakov had trapped him, that life went on. He drove fast, with a dreamy sureness. Near Ansouis he saw Gérard's car coming toward him. They stopped on the road and talked through their open windows. "I'm going to pick up some fresh salmon in Pertuis," Gérard told him. "Why don't you come over this evening?"

14

GEORG DROVE ONTO THE DIRT TRACK, keeping an eye out for the sheep that had been grazing on the steep banks that morning. They had moved on.

He put the car into second and sped up. He had long weaned himself of the habit of going easy on the shock absorbers and exhaust. The sun, the mistral, the sharp smoke of his Gauloise, the pain in his temples from the fourth glass of pastis, the rattling on the washboard gravel path—it all fit perfectly.

He saw the dust whipped up by the other car beyond the bend in the dirt track before he saw or heard it. He wondered how so much dust could rise before it even appeared around the bend. The heavy black Citroën limousine came skidding in the bend and headed straight for Georg. In its wake the dust rose into a wall between the steep banks.

He swerved to the right, but the Citroën didn't move. He honked his horn, heard nothing, waved, and shouted. The other car didn't respond; its windows were tinted, so Georg couldn't see the driver. He slammed on the brakes, swerved even farther toward the side, felt his wheels rattle over the edge. The wipers scraped and stuttered across the dry windshield: he had set them off when he slammed his hand on the horn, and now he tried desperately, as if everything depended on it, to shut them off, to make them stop. He stared at the approaching car, the image of the sky and clouds in the windshield, the scraping wipers that sounded like a rusting bicycle wheel in a ditch.

There was a sharp *bang* as the Citroën drove past. It had swerved out of the way just in time, its side mirror swiping Georg's side mirror and tearing it off. He heard the revving of the other car's engine, the spray of gravel on his car, and through it the explosive sound. Like a gunshot. He sat in his car, his hands shaking, his engine having stalled. For a second the piercing pain in his arm and the blood on his sleeve made him think that he'd been shot. But it was a shard of his mirror that had hit him; it wasn't serious. His every movement was automatic, the shock setting in when he stopped in front of his house a few minutes later, his whole body shaking. Mustering all his willpower, he got out, picked up the mail from the mailbox, opened the gate, went out onto the terrace, sat down on the rocking chair, leaned his head back, and closed his eyes. He craved a cigarette, but didn't have the strength to pull one out of the pack and light it.

After some minutes his nerves steadied and he could unlock the door, get a beer out of the refrigerator, and take it back to the rocking chair. It was cold and good. He enjoyed his cigarette, and only an occasional shudder reminded him of the incident. He rocked in his chair and looked through the mail. There was a letter from his parents, a flyer from the Law Society, and in a thick envelope he found an American paperback: an obscure press was inquiring whether he would translate it. He had offered them his services long ago, but had given up hope. It was a trashy novel, but Georg was pleased.

It was only now, back on the terrace, thinking about work and planning the evening and the following day, that he noticed the cats hadn't come out to greet him. He went into the kitchen, rattled the tins of cat food, filled the bowls, and put them in their usual place. "Snow White, Dopey, Sneezy!"

He went out through the gate. The plums were ripe, the fragrance of lavender in bloom hung in the air, birds twittered and cicadas rasped. There was a gentle breeze. He looked up at the sky. It wasn't going to rain today: he would have to water the herb garden himself. Then he would go to the Bar de l'Étang for an aperitif and have some salmon fettuccine at Les Vieux Temps.

They were lying in the shadow by the garage door; curled up as if asleep, but their eyes and mouths were wide open. A shimmer of blood had seeped into the sandy ground. The bullet holes were in the back of their heads: small, neat holes. Did such a tiny caliber even exist? Had they been killed with air-gun pellets?

He crouched down and caressed them. They were still warm.

The phone rang. He got up slowly, went inside, and picked up the receiver. "Hello?"

It was Bulnakov, his voice serious. "Did you find them?"

"Yes." Georg would have liked to shout threats at him, but he couldn't speak.

"I have already made it clear, Monsieur Polger, that this isn't a game. For the last few days I've been very patient. I waited, hoping you'd see reason. But it seems that you haven't quite grasped the situation. You thought that good old Bulnakov would give up, that he'd turn his back and go on his way. No, Monsieur Polger! Good old Bulnakov will only go on his way when he's got what he wants!" He hung up.

Georg stood there with the receiver in his hand. He understood what Bulnakov had said. He was aware that for the past few days he had lived in an illusion, but didn't know what to do with this awareness. You lie in bed feeling cold, and outside it's even colder: What can you do except pull the thin blanket over you to conserve whatever little heat you have? What use is being aware that the cold is too great and the blanket too thin? Should you tell yourself that you'll freeze to death anyway, and that you might as well get it over with as soon as possible?

But why freeze to death, Georg asked himself. The only thing they want me to do is keep on doing knowingly what I've done up to now unknowingly. I just have to go on with my work and from time to time let Françoise . . . in fact, I don't need to take any action. All I have to do is let things happen. So much in this world isn't the way it ought to be and I look the other way. God knows, the Russians getting the details of the helicopter that the Europeans are building isn't the worst the world has to offer. Perhaps it's even a good thing, creating a balance of power, helping peace. But it's not a matter of what I'm doing: the issue is that I'm being ordered to do it. I haven't accomplished much in life, but at least it can be said that I never did anything I didn't want to do. I might have liked things to be different. But in the end, whatever I did was always my decision. I don't care if that's pride, defiance, independence, or eccentricity.

He hadn't yet grasped that the cats were dead. He knew it, but the knowledge was strangely abstract. As he dug a hole and laid the cats in it, he cried. But as he sat by the living room door staring into the twilight, he felt as if at any moment Dopey would come prancing around the corner.

15

FRANÇOISE KNEW WHAT HAD HAPPENED. "I was there when the two of them showed up. Bulnakov told me to go outside, but I realized what they were up to. My poor darling!"

"You never liked those cats."

"That's not true. Perhaps not as much as you did, but I still liked them." She was leaning against the door frame, running her fingers through his hair.

"Gérard bought some fresh salmon, but I can't say I have much of an appetite. Are you hungry?"

She nestled up to him and put her arm around him. "Why don't we lie down?"

He couldn't make love to her. They lay together in bed, and at first Françoise held him, saying over and over, "My darling, my darling." Then she kissed him and reached to arouse him. But for the first time he found her touch unpleasant. She stopped, rolled onto her stomach, crumpled the pillow under her head, and looked at him. "We still have some champagne in the fridge. How about it?"

"What are we celebrating?"

"Nothing. But it might do us good. And the fact that it's all behind us now. . . . I'm so happy it's all behind us."

"What's behind us?"

"All this nonsense. You and them battling it out. You can't imagine how worried I've been."

Georg sat up. "Are they going away? Have they given up? What have you heard?"

"Them, give up? Never. But you . . . I thought you had . . . well, you don't want . . ." She sat up too, looking at him perplexed. "Don't tell me you still don't get it! They're going to destroy you. They'll do such a good job of it, that . . . They've already killed a man for these stupid plans. We're not talking about three cats now, we're talking about you!"

He looked at her blankly and said despondently, obstinately, "I can't give them those plans."

"Are you crazy?" she shouted. "Don't you care whether you live or die? Life—that's here and now!" She took his hands and put them on her thighs, hips, breasts, and stomach. She wept. "I thought you loved all this. I thought you loved me."

"You know I do." How lame it sounded! She looked at him, disappointed through her tears. As if something beautiful had fallen on the floor and was now lying in pieces.

She didn't go on about how he ought to give Bulnakov the plans. She went to get the champagne, and after the third glass they began to kiss and make love. The next morning she crept out of bed early. When he woke up at seven, she and her car were gone.

He didn't think anything of it. He worked on the translation, and late in the afternoon headed to Cucuron to do some shopping. Then he went to the Bar de l'Étang to see Gérard, and went with him to the wine cooperative at Lourmarin, as he could do with a few bottles himself. It was getting dark when he came home.

He got out of the car and walked toward the house. Suddenly he saw that the door was open. It had been broken open. Inside the house, closets and shelves had been emptied, drawers tipped out, pillows slashed open. The kitchen floor was covered in shattered dishes, cans, oatmeal, spaghetti, cookies, coffee beans, tea bags, tomatoes, eggs. They had gone through everything. He walked through the house, at first stepping carefully amid the books, records, vases, ashtrays, clothes, and papers. But what was the point of watching where he stepped? At times he turned something over with his toe or pushed it out of the way. "Well!" he thought. "There's that telephoto lens I've been looking for everywhere. And it's fine. And there's the Guinness ashtray I thought someone must have swiped."

The plans were still stashed in the drainpipe. He rummaged through the chaos for his dictionaries, the ruler, and a pen, cleared the area in front of his desk, pulled up the chair, and began to work. The translations had to be ready by tomorrow. He would get Françoise to help him clean up later. He was surprised at how unruffled he was.

Françoise didn't appear. At midnight he drove over to Cadenet. The windows of her apartment were dark and her car wasn't there. Maybe she's on her way to my place, he thought. But when he got back home her car wasn't there either.

It was a moonlit night, and as he lay on the fresh sheets covering the slashed mattress he could see the disarray even after he turned out the light. The outlines he was used to seeing from his bed were askew. The small cabinet by the wall on the left lay on its side, and the painting on the right had been taken down. His bed was immersed in a disarray of pants, shorts, jackets, sweaters, and socks. Something lay gleaming among the clothes. He got up to see what it was. A belt buckle.

He couldn't sleep. Just as he wanted to look away from the chaos but couldn't, he also wanted to look away from what Bulnakov had done and what he was still likely to do. And yet there was nothing to be seen. Or there was something to be seen but nothing that could be done about it. To face the disarray meant rolling up his sleeves and putting everything back in its place. But what would it take to face Bulnakov? Getting a gun and shooting him and his henchmen? Georg pulled the blanket up to his chin. I can only hide under the blanket and hope they'll just give up and go away. As for my life—I don't think it would do them much good to kill me.

He got up again and turned on the light. He went downstairs to where he had found the telephoto lens, looked for his camera, which he also found undamaged, and a new roll of film. They've been very systematic, he thought; I just have to look on the floor in front of the appropriate closets and chests of drawers. Georg put the film in the camera and set the alarm clock for six in the morning.

He couldn't shoot those guys, but at least he could photograph them, in case he got involved with the police or wanted to tell someone about all this and needed something to back it up. He knew though that shooting pictures of them was really a substitute for shooting them with a gun.

The following morning at seven-thirty he was already lying in wait in Cadenet. He couldn't keep an eye on both the side-street entrance to the office and the parking lot by the statue of the drummer boy, so he opted for the parking lot. If he could catch them in their cars along with their license plates, perhaps the police might be able to do something with it.

He'd been in Cadenet since seven, had parked his car by the church some distance away, and looked on the square for a place to hide. Street corners, doorways, abutments—but every place where he could get a good view, they could also get a good view of him. Finally he went to the building across from the parking lot and rang the bell of the apartment on the second floor. The family was at the breakfast table. He told them he was a journalist and that he wanted to take pictures of the square in the morning light for *Paris-Match*. They were also eager for him to take some pictures of their building. He promised he would, and they offered him a cup of coffee. He fiddled with the lenses by the window, and began to act as if he were preparing his photo shoot.

That morning, when he had driven past her house, Françoise's car was still not there. At eight he saw it pull into the parking lot. Two men got out. Georg knew them from Bulnakov's office. He was gripped by panic. Had they done something to her? First the cats, then the break-in, and now—oh God!—now Françoise? The men were still standing by the car when Bulnakov arrived. He parked his Lancia but didn't get out, and the two men walked over to him. Georg took one picture after another: Bulnakov resting his arm on the open car window, facing the camera; Bulnakov with the other two standing by his car, then by Françoise's car; and then Bulnakov standing alone in the parking lot, watching the two men drive off in her Deux Cheveaux. If the pictures were to be of any use, he had to have clear shots of the faces, the license plates, and the faces together with the license plates.

Georg drove to Marseille and checked his answering machine for messages. Nothing from Françoise. That evening there was no sign of her, nor was there a note on the door from her. He had bolted shut the broken-down kitchen door and was using the door to the living room to get into the house. Françoise didn't have a key for that door. Might she think he had locked her out and was now furious at him? But she'd still have left him a note. He had called Bulnakov's office a few times, but she hadn't answered. Her car hadn't been in front of her house, and she hadn't opened the door when he rang. The curtains were drawn.

This went on for the next few days. There was no sign of Françoise. He didn't see or hear from Bulnakov or his men. They left his house alone, didn't vandalize his garden or his car, and didn't harm him. Georg spent one more morning in Cadenet, lying in wait. This time he waited at the end of the small side street that led to Bulnakov's office, and photographed them as they entered: Bulnakov himself, the two others, and a young blonde he hadn't seen before. Françoise didn't show up, nor did she go to his place, or to hers, or pick up the phone at Bulnakov's when he called.

In the end Georg was so frayed from waiting for Françoise and his fear for her that he was on the verge of calling Bulnakov and giving in: *You can have it all, I'll send you whatever you want, I'll do whatever you want, steal, copy, take pictures! I just want her back.*

16

IN THE MORNING GEORG WENT TO HIS OFFICE and opened the safe where he kept the originals of the plans, intending to transcribe what he had translated.

The cigarettes were missing—the pack of Gauloises he specifically remembered placing on the plans in the safe the day before yesterday. He always did this; as a smoker, there was nothing worse than being caught short without a cigarette. There were times when he worked late into the night and couldn't buy any downstairs once the bar closed.

It wasn't just about the cigarettes. He had some on him, and even found the pack he'd put on the plans on one of the lower compartments. Someone had gotten into the safe.

His secretary, Chris, Monique, Isabelle? Why would they want to break into the safe? They had all known one another for a long time. They had worked for Maurin long before Georg had, and at better pay. They had come to Provence from elsewhere seeking a quieter life, which they had found with their translation work, and were relieved to be able to work under Georg after Maurin's death. They didn't envy his running the firm, and sometimes poked fun at him for being so industrious. Why should they want to make trouble for him?

Unless Bulnakov had bribed or blackmailed them. We all have our price, Georg thought; it's just a question of the amount. What's surprising is not the number of people being bribed or what they are prepared to do, but for how little most people are prepared to do it. It's a matter of putting the money and morals in relation to each other: when the bribe is high enough, the success is so inevitable that bribery is no longer immoral. What is immoral is selling oneself cheaply. Georg was not angry that his coworkers might let themselves be bribed by Bulnakov for a substantial sum; what annoyed him was that he would have to arrange for a new lock and be more careful. He was relieved, feeling that he and Françoise would no longer be in trouble since Bulnakov had gotten what he wanted. But the question remained: Where had she disappeared to and what had happened to her? Might she be in Marseille, and now assigned to Chris?

He looked out the window. A courtyard, clothes hanging to dry from windows, one newly painted building and paint flaking on others, tall brick chimneys on the roofs. Loud voices of playing children. Beyond the roofs he saw taller buildings and a church tower. Might Françoise be somewhere in this big city waiting for Chris, or getting ready to spend the night. . . . You're crazy, Georg said to himself. These are delusions! You've never seen Chris with a woman. You've often wondered if he's gay.

Things had become easier for Bulnakov's men. When they had searched Georg's house, they had made copies of his office keys. He always left them in the briefcase in which he carried his translation work to and from Marseille. Needless to say, when he'd gone to Cucuron shopping he hadn't taken his briefcase with him. Just you wait, he thought. I'm not going to make things so easy for you, Monsieur Bulnakov! He called a locksmith and had him change the locks on the door and the safe. He urged the locksmith to work as fast as he could, and by evening the job was done. In a store earlier that day he had happened to find a postcard of a tongue sticking out. When he left his office to go to dinner he pinned it to the door.

He stayed the night in Marseille. Mermoz was running late with the new plans, and was going to messenger them over to him the next day. It was a big job, the last of a series. Georg was pleased with the prospect of so much work. The weekend was coming up, the first weekend without Françoise. He didn't believe she would come back. He also didn't believe she was in trouble, or that something had happened to her. It wouldn't make sense, after Bulnakov had gotten hold of all the plans so easily. No, Françoise had simply dropped him. He'd burned his bridges with Bulnakov, and consequently with her too.

He slept on the couch in his office. He had drunk a lot that evening and didn't hear whether or not Bulnakov's men had tried to get in. The next morning the card with the tongue was gone. Though anyone could have taken it.

It was evening by the time Mermoz's messenger came by with two thick rolls of plans and a large batch of construction details and instructions. By the time he had made copies of everything it was getting dark. He had driven the road home so often by day, by night, in heavy traffic, in all weather, even in sleet that he barely noticed the surroundings, until he became aware of a car whose lights stayed behind him. He noticed it on the last part of the highway from Aix to Pertuis, and in Pertuis he tried to shake it. He got away at a red light, which he managed to cross right in front of a big tractor-trailer, and then wove his way through backstreets. But when he got to the road outside town that led to Cucuron they were waiting for him and began tailing him again. Now he knew it was him they were after.

As the road sloped upward he revved his old Peugeot for all it was worth, but the other car followed with ease. He passed other vehicles, but the car tailing him was right behind.

The road beyond Ansouis was empty. He was still driving as fast as he could. He wasn't going to head home but to Cucuron, straight to Les Vieux Temps, where he would honk his horn, bringing everyone out from the restaurant and the bar across the street that was full of billiard- and cardplayers. He wasn't really afraid. He had to concentrate on the road. It was him they were after—his mind went to Bulnakov's men and the plans on the backseat. The postcard of the tongue he had pinned to the door might have made them angry. But what could they do to him on this road from Ansouis to Cucuron, which he had driven a thousand times and where everyone knew him? Perhaps it wasn't them at all, only some idiots playing games.

But it wasn't some idiots playing games. As he came to the dirt track that led to his house, the other car pulled up and swerved toward him, forcing him onto the dirt track. The car swerved again; Georg jammed on the brakes and came to a halt in the ditch, his forehead banging against the steering wheel.

They tore the door open and pulled him out of the car. He was stunned and bleeding from a cut over his eyebrow. As he raised his hand to feel the cut he was punched in the stomach. Then came another punch, and another. He was incapable of even attempting to defend himself. He didn't know where the punches were coming from, how many men were hitting him, or how he could protect himself.

At some point he fell to the ground and lost consciousness. A neighbor found him after he had staggered up, looked in the car, and seen what he knew anyway: the Mermoz plans were gone. He had only been unconscious for a few moments. When he had last checked his watch in Ansouis it was a quarter to ten. Now it was ten. The neighbor insisted on calling the police and an ambulance—"Just look at yourself, just look at yourself!" he kept saying, and Georg looked into his side mirror and saw his blood-stained face. He was in such pain that he could barely stand up.

"No bones broken," the doctor said, after putting some stitches on his eyebrow, "nor any signs of internal injuries. You can go home. Take it easy for a few days."

17

A CUT EYEBROW WILL HEAL, and though bruises are more painful on the second day, they are less so on the third, and after the fourth day just feel like a fading muscle ache. After the police questioned him and drove him home, Georg took a warm bath, and spent much of the weekend in bed and in his hammock. By Sunday he felt strong enough to collect his car and head over to Les Vieux Temps for dinner. Things could have been worse, he told himself; soon everything would be fine. But as the pain subsided, his feeling of helplessness grew. My body, he concluded, whether strong or infirm, is my house, and, like the house I actually live in, is the expression of my integrity. Without my body my integrity is an illusion. That it is here, that I reside in it, that I alone am master of it, is a vital part of being alive; just as the solidity of the ground beneath our feet is an important part of our being alive. He had never thought of it in this way, but now realized that he had felt this way all along. As a boy, during a vacation in Italy, he had experienced an earthquake and realized with dread that there was no depending on the ground on which we stand and walk so confidently. What was worse now than the pain and the horror of being so helpless when they had dragged him out of the car and beat him up was the realization that his body could be ravaged just like his house.

Once every movement no longer hurt and he could walk, bend over, and stretch, he felt anger and hatred. They've taken Françoise away, they've beaten me to a pulp, killed my cats, ransacked my house and my office. They used me, and anything I didn't give them of my own free will they took anyway. If I let them do that, I'm not worth more than a stone or garden hose or cigarette butt. And if it's the last thing I ever do, I'm going to beat the hell out of Bulnakov! I'll blow him up in his car, him and those bastards who did this to me!

He pictured what he would do to them, and how. There was nothing original in his fantasies, just images of avenging heroes from the movies, but when the images ran out and he began to think more clearly, he realized how little he knew. How many people were working for Bulnakov? Where did Bulnakov live, what did he do all day?

On Monday morning Georg drove to Marseille by way of Cadenet. It was a detour, but it took him past Françoise's place. He kept hoping for a sign, a hope he told himself was futile, and for which every disappointment was a confirmation. He no longer went to her apartment.

But her car was there: parked the way she always parked it on the other side of the narrow street, at an angle, only the left wheels on the asphalt, the right ones against the hedge. He pulled up outside the front gate, hurried up the stairs, ran over the gravel, and pressed down on the latch. She never locked the door when she was home. But today the door was locked, and when Georg stepped back confused, he saw that the curtains were still drawn. He knocked on the door, waited, and knocked again.

A truck honked its horn as it carefully edged past Georg's car, which was blocking the road. Somebody called to him from a window in the villa, and he looked up.

"Can I help you?"

"I'm looking for Mademoiselle Kramsky. I see her car is here."

"Mademoiselle Kramsky? She moved out. About a week ago. Ah, the car is back, is it? Well, it's my car, not hers. She rented it from me until today."

"But you said that it was a week ago that she . . ."

"One moment, I'll be right down."

Georg waited by the door. An elderly gentleman in a dressing gown came out.

"Good morning. You are a friend of Mademoiselle's, I believe; I've seen you before. She rented the apartment and the car from me. She wanted to keep the car a little longer so she could go out driving for a few days."

"Do you have her new address?"

"No."

"Then where do you forward her mail?"

"Mail? She never got any."

"I'm sorry to be so insistent, but this is really important. You can't just rent a car like that without having an address."

"That's enough of that, young man. Mademoiselle Kramsky lived here quite a while, and I know whom I can trust. As you said yourself, the car is parked right outside. Good day!"

Georg walked slowly down the stairs and stopped in front of the gate. He took a deep breath. This time the disappointment was not just a confirmation, it hit him full force. His anger was back. He would go to Bulnakov's office and confront him.

He parked his car near the statue of the drummer boy and walked up the rue d'Amazone. The brass plaque next to the bell was no longer there—it was the right building, but the plaque was gone. A man in white overalls came walking up the street, told

Georg the door was open, and went inside. Georg followed him up to the third floor. The door stood open. Here, too, Bulnakov's plaque was gone, and the painters were at work.

"What's going on?" Georg asked the man he had followed up the stairs.

"What does it look like? We're painting." He was a young man with a cheerful, cheeky face, who had been whistling all the way up the stairs.

"What about the people who had the office here?"

"Monsieur Bulnakov? He's the one who hired us." He laughed. "He paid us too."

"Do you know the landlord or the owner of the building?"

"Oh, are you thinking of renting the place? Monsieur Placard lives on the ground floor."

Georg knew what Monsieur Placard would say: Monsieur Bulnakov hadn't left a forwarding address or any other contact information. Saturday afternoon he and some other men had vacated the premises. "He gave me all the furniture. My son and I brought it down to the cellar. Might you be interested in it?"

"In office furniture?" Georg shook his head and left. Like a nightmare, he thought, but like a nightmare it's gone away.

18

BUT NOW HIS WHOLE LIFE TURNED into a nightmare.

It was at the office that Georg first noticed that everything had changed. The Mermoz job, for which he had been beaten up, had not only been the last in a series, but the very last. No more jobs came. He called Mermoz and asked what the matter was, but was put off. When he called again, he was told in no uncertain terms that Mermoz was no longer interested in his services. All his major accounts began to dry up, one after the other. Within a month his agency was ruined. Not that there weren't any translation jobs, but there wasn't even enough work to cover the rent or pay the secretary.

Then his problems with the police began. They had initially accepted that he didn't know who had attacked him or why. The two officers who took his statement had been pleasant and sympathetic. But a few weeks later two other officers showed up. They wanted to know the exact particulars of the accident, the route he'd taken, what he had in his car. They asked him for his opinion about the attack: If he were going to rob anyone, would he choose to rob someone driving an old Peugeot? Why he had moved from Karlsruhe to Cucuron? What did he do for a living? What had he done for a living in Germany? No, they couldn't drop the matter. They kept coming back, sometimes two officers, sometimes one, always asking the same questions.

The policeman in Cucuron also had his eye on him. The little town had only one policeman, everybody knew him and he knew everybody. Nobody held it against him when he took it upon himself to have a car towed that someone had left in the middle of the street in a drunken stupor, or if he stopped someone from burning trash in their backyard, or had a door broken down for the bailiff. Can one blame a dentist if he drills and there is pain? And like a dentist, Cucuron's policeman didn't inflict pain without good reason.

At first Georg wasn't particularly concerned when the policeman didn't return his greeting. I suppose he didn't see me or didn't recognize me, he thought, or maybe his mind was elsewhere, or perhaps he mistook me for one of those tourists passing through Cucuron.

One day he was sitting at a table outside the Bar de l'Étang. Gérard and Nadine were with him, and the bartender had come out to sit with them. The other tables were full too, as the morning market was over. He had parked his car where he always did, and where everyone else did too: among the old plane trees by the pond.

"Is that your car?" the policeman asked, towering before Georg and pointing at his yellow Peugeot.

"It is, but . . ." Georg wanted to reply that he knew well enough it was his car, and ask him what this was all about.

"You can't leave your car there."

Georg was more taken aback than outraged. "Why not? Everyone parks there."

"I repeat, you'll have to move your car." The policeman had raised his voice, and everyone at the surrounding tables was watching and listening. Georg looked at the curious and indifferent faces. The bartender got up and went back behind the bar. Gérard stirred his espresso, avoiding Georg's eyes. Nadine was fidgeting with her bag.

Georg controlled himself. "Could you tell me why I can't leave my car there?"

"I will not repeat myself. Move it now."

Georg again looked at the people sitting at the tables. He knew most of them, had chatted with many of them, played billiards or table-top football, had drunk Pernod with them. After two years in Cucuron, he felt that he belonged here, particularly now in summer when flocks of tourists were milling about the town. But he didn't belong. There was spite in the faces, not just the indifference of not wanting to get involved. Georg got up and went over to his car. It was like running a gauntlet. He didn't look for another parking spot, but drove home.

From that day on everyone's behavior toward him changed: the baker, the butcher, the grocer, and the people he met in the post office, in the bar, and on the street. Or was he imagining things? The quick looking away that obviated the need to greet or be greeted, the slight hesitation of the baker's wife from whom he bought a loaf of bread, the hint of condescension with which the café owner took his order. He couldn't have proven any of this in court, but he felt it. What surprised him the least was that the branch manager of his bank asked him to step into his office. For months there had been a lot of activity in his account, and now there were no more deposits, only withdrawals. Needless to say, the bank had to check that everything was as it should be. As for his landlord—he had always been something of a psychopath. That he drove around his house every evening in his old Simca might have something to do with it. But now there were phone calls from the landlord's wife, who had always been reasonable in the past. They were sorry, but their daughter was coming back from

Marseille and wanted to move into Georg's house. They would have to discuss terminating his four-year lease early.

Georg had nothing to say to any of this. All his strength, courage, and trust were gone. I'm an open wound, he thought.

There was nothing left with which he could ease his thoughts and longing for Françoise.

He was furious: *I gave you my love and you took it, but for you it was only physical. You enjoyed our nights together as much as I did, gave yourself to me with as much abandon and pleasure as I gave myself to you. For me the passion I gave and took was a seal on our love, but for you it was only a passion each partner kindles and satisfies, a passion that doesn't seal anything. If I could have been so wrong, if you could have deceived me like that, if such devotion cannot even act as a seal of love—what's left for me to believe in? How am I supposed to ever love again?* One silent reproach followed another. But even the most absurd accusations couldn't bring her back. When someone leaves us, we accuse them so that they apologize and come back. In this way we are serious about the accusations, but are ready to agree to any conditions. Georg was aware of that.

He tried to be reasonable. The pain of separation is just a phantom pain, he told himself. How can something that no longer exists hurt me? Yet the slightest circumstance taught him that a phantom pain is not just phantom, but in fact real pain. He was sitting in the restaurant, had eaten well, was having a glass of Calvados and a cigarette, and suddenly imagined her sitting across from him, sighing contentedly, leaning back, and rubbing her tummy. He had always felt uncomfortable when she did this. But now, even this image stung. Or he found a long brown hair in the basin, which unleashed cascades of beautiful memories, though in the past, when he found a hair of hers in the basin, it had always irritated him.

He toyed with cynical quips that he found elegant or that

sounded clever. *One can't end a relationship by splitting up. One must continue in the relationship and weave it into the tapestry of one's life, or forget the relationship. Forgetting is the garbage dump of life. I'm throwing you into the garbage, Françoise!*

None of that changed the fact that he missed her. When he woke up, sat down at the breakfast table, busied himself with the herb garden, and felt the empty house behind him; when he walked along the paths the two of them had walked; when—everyone has experienced something similar. He no longer had anything to do. He lived off the rest of the money that had come in so lavishly over the past few months. What he would do when it ran out, he didn't know. He couldn't think about that. He often sat all afternoon in the rocking chair, staring blankly at the trees.

19

IN SEPTEMBER AN OLD FRIEND FROM HEIDELBERG came to visit. The first evening they stayed up late, lit a fire in the fireplace after midnight, and opened a bottle of wine.

"Do you want to hear a crazy story?" Georg asked, and told him what had happened.

"I only saw Françoise that one time when you invited us all to your party," his friend said. "Do you have any pictures of her?"

"I took a lot of pictures, but she either took them with her or they got lost when my place was ransacked. I only have one left." He got up and went to find it. It was a picture of Françoise on a couch in her apartment, reading, her eyes downcast.

"Ah yes. By the way, what's that picture on her wall?"

"It's the cathedral in Warsaw where her parents were married."

A short while later, Georg's friend asked to see the photograph again.

"It isn't a particularly good one," Georg said. "She didn't like being photographed, so I often took snapshots of her when she wasn't looking. Though some of the pictures did turn out quite . . ."

"That's not in Warsaw. I know that church. I can't think of its name. It's in New York."

Georg looked at him in surprise. "Why would she have a picture from New York on her wall?"

"No idea. All I know is that it's in New York, a cathedral they never finished that's still under construction. St. John! That's it! It's enormous! I think it's the biggest church in the world after St. Peter's."

"New York . . ." Georg shook his head.

Over the next few days Georg kept coming back to the subject. "Are you sure that the cathedral in the picture is in New York?"

"Well, perhaps Warsaw has the same one. In Wiesbaden there's a cathedral that was built from Schinkel's plans. Wiesbaden's municipal architect had purchased the plans in Berlin, and there's probably a church just like it somewhere in Berlin. But as for America, it's a bit hard to imagine. The Americans would sooner have copied Chartres than Warsaw, and as for the Poles constructing their churches along American designs—you tell me if that makes sense."

The evening before his friend left, Georg asked him if he knew anyone in New York who might put him up for a while.

"I'll give it a try."

"Please, it's important."

"You mean now?"

"I put in a call to a travel agent this morning," Georg told him. "I'm flying next week from Brussels."

"For how long?"

"Until I find her."

"It's a big city," his friend said dubiously.

"I know. I also know that Françoise could be anywhere in the world. But why did she lie about the picture?"

"You don't know where she got it. Maybe she herself didn't know where it was from."

Georg looked at him irritated. "You've seen for yourself the kind of life I'm leading. What am I supposed to do here? I'd rather take the money I still have and . . . I don't know how I'll look for her, but I'll think of something."

After his friend had left, Georg sold what he could sell, and threw away whatever didn't fit in his car and nobody wanted.

A week later he gave the landlord the keys to his empty house.

Part Two

20

GEORG SET OUT LATE IN THE AFTERNOON and drove all night. He missed the turnoff to Paris at Beaune, and the highway ended at Dijon. He drove along back roads, past Troyes and Reims. The bends in the road kept him awake. He sped through dark towns and villages, where yellow lights bathed the streets in a dim haze. He slowed down at the brightly lit pedestrian crossings. Sometimes he waited at an empty intersection for the light to change. There was nobody in the streets and hardly any cars. In Reims he found an open gas station; the fuel light had been blinking for some time. He drove past the cathedral. The facade reminded him of the picture in Françoise's room.

After a painfully slow border crossing, where the French customs officer grilled him on where he was coming from and where he was heading, he got back on the highway at Mons. By seventhirty in the morning he was at his friends' place in Brussels. The house was bustling. Felix was getting ready to leave for work, and Gisela was heading to the station to catch a train for Luxembourg, where she worked as an interpreter for the European parliament. The older of their two boys was off to kindergarten. Georg was warmly welcomed, but then quickly forgotten in the breakfast rush, with the babysitter arriving and everyone else leaving. Gisela told him that of course he could leave his car there, and gave him a quick hug. "Good luck in America," she said. She saw something in his face. "Is everything all right?" Then she was gone.

The babysitter drove him to the airport. In the plane, he felt frightened for the first time. He had thought he was only leaving Cucuron, where he had nothing left to lose. Now he felt as if he were giving up his whole life.

It was a budget flight, with narrow seats and no drinks or food. No movie, either. He had intended to save money on the earphones, had looked forward to the distraction of the images on the screen. He gazed out the window at the clouds over the Atlantic, fell asleep, and woke up hours later. His neck, back, and legs were aching. The sun was setting behind red clouds, a picture of lifeless beauty. By the time the plane landed in Newark it was dark.

It took him two hours to get through customs, find the bus to New York, and arrive at the Port Authority bus terminal. He took a cab. There was a lot of traffic, even at eleven at night. The driver swore in Spanish, drove too fast, and kept slamming on the brakes. After a while, the cab drove up an avenue with tall buildings on the left and dark trees on the right. Georg felt a rush of excitement. This had to be Central Park, and the avenue Central Park West. The cab pulled up. He had arrived. There was a green baldachin from the edge of the sidewalk to the entrance.

Georg opened the door, went in, and found himself standing in a vestibule. A guard sat reading at a desk behind a glass door. Georg knocked once, then twice. The man pointed at the wall next to Georg. There was a bronze panel with an alphabetical list of names and corresponding apartment numbers, and an intercom. Georg picked up the receiver, the line crackling as if he were making a transatlantic call. "Hello?" said the guard's voice, and Georg gave his name and introduced himself as Mr. and Mrs. Epp's guest.

The guard buzzed him in, gave him the key to the apartment, and told him where it was. The elevator had two doors: on the sixth floor Georg kept standing before the elevator door through which he had entered, until he realized that the door behind him had opened. He was exhausted. Back in France, day was breaking over the Luberon.

The apartment was the one next to the elevator. It took him a while to figure out how to unlock all three locks. He had to turn the keys in the opposite direction from what he was used to. The door was heavy, and fell shut behind him with a contented *click*. He found the guest room at the end of the long hall. Near the front door was a study where he found some telephone directories. Françoise Kramsky? No, as was to be expected, there was no listing under that name. He looked for the church.

In the White Pages he found neither a John, nor a St. John, nor a Church of St. John. There was more than a column of churches, from the Church of All Nations to the Church of the Truth. But the listings seemed to be random. In the Yellow Pages, between Christmas Trees and Cigarettes, he found a listing of churches by denomination. He was certain that a church destined to become the biggest in the world after St. Peter's wouldn't belong to a minor denomination, and so concentrated on the Episcopalian, Lutheran, and Catholic churches. The tiny letters blurred before his tired eyes, whirled around, found themselves again in long rows, and marched down the column of listings.

CATHEDRAL CHURCH OF ST. JOHN THE DIVINE. The name was in larger print, and in bold. Amsterdam Avenue and 112th Street. There was a map on the wall of the study. He found the cathedral and also located the Epps' apartment. It wasn't too far away. Georg felt as if he had made it.

21

HE WOKE UP ON THE COUCH in the study, still dressed, curled up and aching. He crossed the hall to the living room. The sun cast a broad band of rays through the large windows. He looked out. Below him was a stream of traffic, and across the street lay Central Park. Skyscrapers in the distance towered into the clear blue sky of Manhattan. He opened the window and heard the noise of the traffic, the clattering of the subway under the street, and the children in the playground at the edge of the park.

Outside, he drank in the atmosphere of the city. He walked uptown along Amsterdam Avenue. The buildings, at first tall and well maintained, shrank into four- and five-story houses. Fire escapes hung black and heavy into the streets. The stores had signs in Spanish. The streets became louder and more lively. The pedestrians were increasingly black and Latino; there were more drunks, panhandlers, and teenagers carrying boom boxes. He walked fast, his eyes flitting over buildings, people, cars, traffic lights, hydrants, mailboxes.

Georg didn't see the cathedral until he reached the intersection. The cross street was flanked by low Gothic buildings, behind which the massive gray cathedral rose up. He crossed the street and took out the photograph of Françoise with the print of the cathedral hanging on the wall behind her. He compared it to the building in front of him. The towers to the right and left of the portal only reached the height of the nave, and the cupola over the crossing was still in bare cement, but otherwise everything matched perfectly. Steps stretching the whole breadth of the cathedral led up from Amsterdam Avenue to the five portals.

The inside was gloomy and steeped in secrets, the dim light coming from lamps and the stained-glass windows. The columns faded upward into the darkness. He walked through the nave with the respect his parents had always shown on entering a church. Only the area around the choir stalls was brighter. He found the gift shop on the left, and strolled among the display cases and tables, his eyes scanning the books and cards, soaps, fruit preserves, sweatshirts, bags, and cups, until he came upon a large print. He recognized it. Françoise had cut off the lower part where it said: THE CATHEDRAL OF SAINT JOHN THE DIVINE. MORNINGSIDE HEIGHTS IN THE CITY OF NEW YORK. CRAM AND FERGUSON, HOYLE, DORAN AND BERRY, ARCHITECTS, BOSTON. It was the front view of the west facade. He kept reading the text over and over as if it might reveal something.

On his way back to the entrance he sat down. Now what? Did this mean that Françoise was living in New York, or just that she had lived here before? Someone could have given her the print as a present, or she could have bought it at a flea market or in a junk store. She had cut off the reference to New York, but it wasn't clear whether she was trying to cover something up or whether she just didn't want the text. If she had been in New York but was no longer here, he might as well look for her in Paris, Sydney, or San Francisco. But even if she was in New York, it would be like looking for a needle in a haystack.

His eyes had adjusted to the dim light. The distant voices he heard came from a tour group visiting the cathedral. The chairs in the row were battered, some with frayed wickerwork. The columns no longer melted into the darkness above, but were supporting a ribbed vault. No secrets—just bad lighting, gloomy corners, empty space, and distorted acoustics. But no secrets.

He got up and went back to the gift shop. He showed the cashier Françoise's picture, an enlarged close-up of her reading on the bed. "Do you happen to know her?"

The young woman looked at him cautiously. "What do you want? Who are you?"

He had conjured up a romantic story: Françoise had visited Europe, their meeting in France, their love, a silly lover's quarrel in which he had walked out in a huff, his not being able to find her. He looked the cashier in the eye and then lowered his gaze: such a foolish quarrel, his foolish pride, his foolish temper, he was ashamed of himself. Then he raised his eyes again with a sincere and determined look. "I've come to ask her to marry me."

Since the cashier had not been working there very long, she took him to her boss, who had been the manager for ten years. The manager didn't remember ever seeing Françoise either, but all that meant was that Françoise hadn't worked there during the past ten years. Whether she had been a customer was another question— that, she couldn't say. She herself wasn't always on the floor, and she'd had many shop assistants over the years.

22

GEORG WAS NEVER SURE whether people were won over by his tale because they believed it, or because he was so sincere. Besides his romantic tale he also had one in which he was a young lawyer and Françoise an acquaintance of a client in France who didn't know her full name or address. She was to be a key witness in a trial, the trial was vital for the client, and the client vital for Georg, who was an up-and-coming lawyer. What people liked about both tales was the role played by the picture of the cathedral, their cathedral. They looked at the photo carefully, gave the matter some thought, said they were sorry they couldn't help him, and sometimes suggested where he might look further.

He spoke to current and former priests connected with the cathedral, with parishioners who had been volunteers, with the head of the Ladies Guild, the head of the theater workshop. Nobody recognized the face in the photograph. At times he felt her face becoming more unfamiliar to him every time he took out the picture and showed it. Was this the face that had smiled at him, that he had seen from so close, and touched and kissed? He felt that his growing unfamiliarity had to do with Françoise's lowered eyes. But perhaps it would be even worse if her eyes had been visible. Maybe they, too, would wear away as he kept taking out the picture and showing it around. Usually the past lurks unnoticed behind the present, but Georg felt as if the past was being slowly sucked away under his helpless gaze.

In two weeks he had met over twenty people. He now knew the Upper West Side where most of them lived, and the subways and buses that took him to those who lived in other places. He knew the baroque, putto-decorated entrance of the Polish consulate, and the cold, white facade of the Soviet one. He often stood outside, or sat on a stoop across from the grand townhouse of the Poles or on the steps of the synagogue that the Russians eyed with grim faces. He didn't know whether secret-service agents reported to their consulates, but a consulate offers a connection between its nation and the host nation, and Georg was seeking just such a relationship in the hope of finding out more about Françoise or even Bulnakov. He went inside both consulates and asked for Françoise Kramsky's address, telling the staff he believed she had once either worked there or was somehow connected to the consulate. Both the Poles and the Russians told him they were not at liberty to provide that kind of information. He told them his tales in vain. He showed the officials her picture, but their faces betrayed no reaction.

He experienced Manhattan as a forest. This city isn't on an island, he thought, it is an island. It isn't part of a landscape, it is the landscape, a landscape of stone vegetation alien to its people, who must first hack paths through it and build dwellings that always risked being overwhelmed by the vegetation. Sometimes he came upon burned-out shells of buildings, lots heaped with rubble, facades with windows and doors that were empty or bricked up. It was as if they had been ravaged by war—but since there had been no war, it was as if nature had reclaimed them: not a rampant forest but a raging earthquake. The new buildings towered into the sky like growing crystals.

At night he had weird dreams. Many days he didn't talk to a soul.

His money was running out. He only had a thousand dollars left, which wouldn't last long in New York. The Epps gave him to understand, pleasantly but firmly, that it was time he moved on. He had gotten nowhere. Should he give up?

He sat in the Hungarian Pastry Shop, a café across from the cathedral. One could sit there as long as one liked. They served homemade cookies, and there were free coffee refills. The air was heavy with smoke. The paintings in the café were ugly, its mirrors dull; the paint was flaking off the walls and the column in the center of the room, beside which was a chest of drawers with a jug of coffee on top. The shop was a refuge for those who hadn't yet made it or who no longer had any prospects of making it. Georg came here to relax and do some thinking. He exchanged a few words with people sitting at nearby tables, borrowed a newspaper, was asked for a light, or offered a cigarette.

Two men at the next table were talking about apartments and rents. One of them, Larry, was looking for a roommate. Georg told him he was looking for a place, and Larry said he had a room he could have for four hundred dollars. Larry taught German at Columbia, and liked the idea of having a German roommate. Within minutes everything was settled, and later that day Georg moved in.

He had the corner room of a twelfth-floor apartment, whose two windows looked out on different parts of the city. One faced a church tower, backyards, fire escapes, and rooftops, and had an uptown view of Broadway until the haze of the day swallowed the cars and houses, and the darkness of night swallowed their lights. His sleep was pierced by the howl of sirens, feverish spirals of sound that began and ended with a high-pitched gasp. From the other window he looked out onto a parking lot, low buildings, the trees of Riverside Park, and the Hudson River, lying wide and idle with its metallic sheen in the sun, and in bad weather melting into the opposite bank. From time to time a barge plowed its waters. The sun set between the wooden water towers on the roofs. The window facing west was larger, and the view from it wider. At times Georg felt as if he could spread out his arms and fling himself out over the parking lot, gliding over houses and trees and over the Hudson, and land like a large bird on the water. Why should he, who only had to spread out his arms in order to fly, give up his search?

Georg still hadn't seen one of the former coordinators of the theater workshop or the former head of the Ladies Guild who was now running the kindergarten. He called and made appointments. Calvin Cope, the former director of the cathedral's theater workshop, was now a real director, and initially said he was too busy to meet. It was a matter of life and death? he asked. Georg had crossed the Atlantic, come all the way from Europe? Well, in that case he'd meet him for lunch at a place on Fifty-second Street.

23

THE RESTAURANT SOUNDED EXPENSIVE, and Georg borrowed a jacket and tie from Larry, his roommate. The coat check and bar were at street level, and the maître d' escorted Georg upstairs, where a table by the window had been reserved for Mr. Cope.

Georg ordered a glass of white wine and gazed out at the street. The traffic flowed by in a slow stream; there were many yellow cabs, and the occasional black limousine with tinted windows and a TV antenna on its trunk. It began to rain. A street hawker appeared on the opposite sidewalk, selling umbrellas. A young man with shining red hair, holding his coat collar up, stood huddling by the entrance of a shoe store with a large display window that exhibited only one or two pairs of shoes on tiled stands.

The waiter brought an elderly gentleman and a young woman to the table and pulled out chairs for them.

"Mr. Cope?" Georg said, standing up.

"This is the European romantic I was telling you about, Lucy, the one who followed his sweetheart across the ocean!"

They sat down. Georg couldn't take his eyes off Lucy. She was a beauty, an American beauty. Her face was sculptured, with high cheekbones, a strong chin, deep-set eyes, and a childlike mouth with full lips. She was slender, but with wide shoulders and big breasts. He had first noticed such women in commercials, and then had seen them on the street too. He had often wondered what gave them that special something that made them stand apart from European women. He looked at her and still couldn't figure it out.

Cope eyed him with amusement. "She's very beautiful and young, and destined to be a marvelous actress."

"I'm springtime and Calvin is autumn," Lucy said laughing, and by the time Georg thought of the compliment that he would consider himself lucky to be such an autumn, the moment had passed. The compliment would have been quite sincere, not only because of Lucy, but also because Cope obviously took great pleasure in his maturity and lifestyle. He had a full head of gray hair, and peered at the menu over his spectacles with a senatorial air.

"Leave the ordering to me," Cope said. "I've been coming here for years. In the meantime, aren't you going to say something?"

Georg hadn't said a word yet. "I'm very grateful you have taken the time to see me, Mr. Cope. I don't even know her real name: she wanted me to call her Françoise, as it's a French name and she loves France. But I do know," he lied smoothly, "that she was involved with the cathedral's theater workshop and that she had a great teacher. She often spoke of it. This rather bad picture is the only thing I have." Georg took out the photo and gave it to Cope, who passed it on to Lucy and looked at Georg pensively.

"Isn't there a German poem about a woman searching for someone?" Cope asked. "All she knows is his name, and she follows him across the sea? Or is it the other way around, he follows her? My mother's Swiss. She used to recite that poem when I was a boy."

"Do you speak German?"

"I used to. But that poem—your touching story reminded me

of it when we were talking on the phone. Do you know the one I mean?"

"*Am Gestade Palästinas, auf und nieder, Tag um Tag . . .*" Georg began.

"That's it! I remember it now. Do you know the whole poem?"

"No, but I remember a Saracen maiden who follows a man to London, and then, lost in the crowds of the city, calls out 'Gilbert' and finds him. The man had been captured in one of the Crusades, and she had freed him. She only knew two English words: 'Gilbert' and 'London.' The poem says that love will cross the seas even with only two words. We learned it at school."

"Well, let's drink to that," Cope said, raising his glass. "Now, let me see the picture."

Lucy gave him the photo.

"What's that poem about?" she asked Georg. "I didn't quite understand." She spoke in a soft American English, as if chewing on a potato. Georg told her about the poem and about Conrad Ferdinand Meyer and about his grandparents, who had lived by the lake in Zurich.

"I recognize the face," Cope said suddenly. "That girl used to be in my workshop, but I just can't remember her name." He continued studying the photograph. "I'm not sure who might know. I never kept records. I have a good eye for faces and have never had trouble remembering who was paid up and who still owed me— not to mention that I always gave the students in my class new names."

"Yes, they're names that suit them," Lucy said. "Calvin still does that, and most of the actors like it, and then keep it as a stage name."

"But I know that you don't like the name I gave you," Cope said to her, "and autumn wouldn't pick a fight with beautiful spring over a name, would he, which is why you are Lucy, nothing but Lucy, forever Lucy." He laughed, but Georg wasn't sure if there might be a touch of poison in his joviality.

The Châteaubriand arrived, was carved up, and served.

"Do you perhaps remember any of the other members of the workshop from back then?"

"No, I'm sorry, I can't recall anyone. It's been five or six years. You're lucky I have such a good memory for faces, since this picture here is quite bad—was it you who took it? It's no use. I'm sorry, but you'll have to follow the example of the Saracen maiden. You crossed the ocean and came to New York convinced you'd find her, and now you'll have to walk the streets of New York with the same conviction."

Georg thought that sounded snide. Was Cope's joviality indeed poisoned? Was he somehow irritated? Georg glanced out of the window. It wasn't raining anymore, but the red-haired man was still standing in the doorway across the street. They ate in silence.

"Are you working on a new piece?" Georg asked in order to start a conversation.

"Why do you want to know? What do you know about the theater? What is all this? Goddamn it, nothing but idiots everywhere! First Goldberg, then Sheldon, and now this crazy lovebird from Europe!" Cope's voice had gotten louder.

The waiter was more amused than put out, and seemed to be used to Cope's scenes. Lucy put down her knife and fork, took a hairpin out of her bag, gathered her long, thick brown hair with both hands into a bun, and stuck it fast.

"Let's go, I've had enough of this!" Cope shouted. "Waiter! Put the meal on my tab!" He jumped up and hurried down the stairs.

"It was nice meeting you," Lucy said with a smile. "Can you write your name down? I can send you a ticket for opening night. I wouldn't take any of this too seriously."

Georg sat alone at the table in front of all the full plates. The waiter took the bottle out of the ice bucket and poured more wine. Georg ate the entire Châteaubriand and all the side orders and finished the bottle. The waiter brought him an espresso without asking if he wanted one and Georg ordered a brandy. He was celebrating. Françoise really had been in New York.

24

GEORG HAD NEVER BEEN SHADOWED BEFORE. Was it a coincidence that the red-haired man he'd seen from the restaurant window was now also strolling around the skating rink at Rockefeller Center? Georg stopped in front of boutiques, seeking the reflection of the street in the display windows, sometimes quickly glancing back. He knew this from the movies. He went into a bookstore and stood in the aisles, blindly leafing through books. It didn't work: he could only keep the street in sight by standing next to the cashier. He went outside. It had started to rain again. There was a light gray haze around the tops of the skyscrapers, projectors throwing streams of light into the low-hanging clouds. Raindrops fell on his glasses. He looked up and felt as if he were soaring into a deep and starry sky, like the crane shot at the opening of some movies. The traffic was heavy, with a swarm of yellow cabs and crowds of people walking fast. Somebody bumped into him and he almost fell. He turned around, and though he didn't see who had run into him, he caught sight of the red-haired man, who was now only a few yards behind him—he too without an umbrella, his wet hair plastered to his head.

Late in the afternoon of the following day Georg saw the young man again. He had been looking through old telephone directories for a bona fide Kramsky, perhaps a friend, a relative, or even a former coworker whose name Françoise might have borrowed. He hadn't found anything. At five o'clock he had left the New York Public Library on Forty-second Street and walked uptown. Where should he look next? The theater workshops at the cathedral changed every year, but perhaps some of the participants signed up several years in a row. He could ask the members of the current workshop if anyone had been a member of a previous one and might know someone who had been a member of an even earlier one, who, in turn, might know someone who had . . . On Madison Avenue Georg eyed the expensive trifles that filled the display windows of the boutiques: flowers, paintings, jewelry, toys, antiques, expensive carpets. The women with their elegant clothes and comportment looked at him coldly, as if they were gingerly picking up some bauble, glancing at it, and casting it aside.

A bus stop sign listed a bus that went past Georg's place. He turned to look if he could see a bus coming, and saw the redhead again. He was on the other side of the street, and turned to look at a store window. The bus arrived, but the redhead made no sign of getting on too. For as long as Georg could see him from the bus, the man was still looking into the shop windows.

People were getting on and off, people were shopping, a fire hydrant was being given a fresh coat of paint, store shutters were being repaired, a car was being unloaded, two people were embracing next to a waiting cab. Georg saw all this but didn't take it in. It was all about winners and losers. He and those like him stood on one side: amateurs, fools, and losers; on the other side were the professionals who were part of the world of big business, international politics, organized crime, and the secret service: the world of success. Still, like anyone who reads the newspapers, he had seen enough politicians and businessmen trip and fall over their lies and blunders. But what intimidated him about the redhead's shadowing him was how amateurishly he seemed to go about it.

The bus went up Madison Avenue and turned left. He had a hard time finding his bearings. At the next bus stop he saw on his left the bleak northern end of Central Park, and on his right a row of bricked-up, dilapidated mansions that had once been beautiful. Black children were playing in the rays of an early streetlight. A girl of about ten seemed to be putting on some kind of show: she struck poses like a star, limped like an old woman, scolded a little boy as if she were his mother, and strutted about like a macho guy putting the moves on a beautiful woman. She dropped the act, but the bus moved on and Georg couldn't see what she did next.

25

WHEN GEORG OPENED THE DOOR to his apartment, he heard music, voices, and laughter. Two children were playing in the hall, and there were some people sitting in the living room, though most of the guests had crowded into the kitchen. Larry had given a lecture on Kafka in America that had been very well received, and was now throwing a party for his friends and his colleagues from the German Department.

Georg poured himself a drink and mingled with the guests. In the kitchen he heard scraps of English and German conversations, academic chitchat. A beautiful, vain woman with black hair and green stockings was leaning against the door. "How are you?" Georg asked, but she turned away and began talking to a young man in a turquoise shirt.

An amicable elderly gentleman in a purple jacket and a violet scarf asked Georg whether they had met before. They hadn't.

A black man in a white suit asked Georg what he was doing in New York, and Georg told him he was working on a book. The black man introduced himself as a reporter for the *New York Times,* and said he was still waiting for his big break. One day he'd make a real splash with a big feature.

In the living room a man was telling a story to a captive audience. "Finally our lawyers came to an agreement," he was saying. "She gets custody, and I get visiting rights every Sunday." Everyone laughed.

"What's so funny?" Georg whispered to a woman next to him.

"Every time I come back," the man continued, "I'm a shadow of my former self." Again everyone laughed, except for the man telling the story; he was spindly and of an uncertain age, with sparse curls and nervous fingers.

"That's Max," the woman next to Georg whispered, as if in answer to his previous question.

"And?"

She took Georg aside. "The dog . . . Max and his girlfriend broke up and have been fighting over who gets to keep the dog. By the way, my name is Helen. Who are you?" She looked up at him expectantly. She was short and wearing a tight skirt and a thick woolen pullover out of which peeked the collar of her blouse. She struck him as having wary eyes. He wasn't certain whether they were defensive or unsure. She had longish, dark blond hair, and one eyebrow arched slightly higher than the other. Her mouth was set and her chin energetic.

"I'm Georg, Larry's new roommate. Are you in the German Department too?"

She was teaching German and was working on a dissertation about German fairy tales, and had lived in Germany for quite a while as a student. She spoke fluent German, and only hesitated sometimes searching for a word, because it had to be just right.

"So you're interested in the cathedral?" she asked. "Larry calls you the . . ." She tried to find the right expression, "the cathedral researcher."

"Cathedral researcher? Not much of a topic. No, I'm here to . . .

Where's your glass? I'm going to get myself some more wine—would you like some too?"

She was waiting for him when he got back with the bottle and the glasses. She talked about her work on her thesis, and about her cat, Effi. She asked him if the German word *Alraune* had the same mysterious connotation as *mandrake* had in English. She told him the tale of a man who pulls a mandrake root from the soil, hears a plaintive, earthshaking cry, and suddenly finds a magician standing in front of him. Georg conjectured about the connection between the words *Alraunen, runes,* and the German word *raunen,* "to whisper." He told her about France and his take on the French, what he liked about New York, and what he found intimidating about it. He could share with Helen his fairy-tale fears. Her conversation was clever and witty, and she listened to him attentively.

Georg was touched. He hadn't had a normal conversation in ages, especially not with a woman. He had enjoyed talking with Françoise, though they had never talked extensively. But after he had caught her with a camera in his study that night, he had mistrusted her words and had calculated his, and their communication had become artificial. Slowly his trust in the normality of communication with others had been frayed, first with Bulnakov and Françoise, and then with his translators in Marseille and his friends in Cucuron. He remembered the evening he had dropped by Les Vieux Temps to have some salmon fettuccine. Gérard had greeted him warmly—too warmly. Had Gérard been lying in wait for him? Georg had abruptly turned back at the door and left, after which he had avoided Gérard.

Georg longed to have faith—not in some higher power, but in day-to-day things one could rely on. But could he trust Helen? Had he drawn her into a conversation or had she drawn him? He had met her at Larry's and he had met Larry at the Hungarian

Pastry Shop. Were these coincidences, or some strategy? Was Bulnakov behind Larry and Helen, behind the red-haired man? Georg was no longer listening to what Helen was saying, and had a hard time coming across as if he were listening at all. What could he tell her about himself without actually saying anything? He made small talk, nodded as she spoke, laughed, shook his head, asked her this and that, and was happy when he had the opportunity to look down at the floor for a few moments to gather his thoughts. All this took a lot out of him.

He excused himself and went to the toilet. When he got back, she was no longer there. In his room he went and stood by the window. He felt a lump rising from his chest to his throat. How will I ever be able to love anyone again? How can I learn once more to interact normally with people? I'm going insane, really insane. He began to cry and felt better, though the lump in his throat didn't dissolve.

One of the guests came bursting into the room. Larry had put all the coats on Georg's bed. Georg blew his nose. Other guests came and collected their things. The party was over. Before she left, Helen asked him if he wanted to meet Effi. She sounded natural and friendly. His suspicion was once more aroused. Effi? Who was this Effi? Oh, of course! Effi was her cat. He laughed and they set a date.

26

GEORG LAY ON HIS BED and looked out the window. It was dawn, the sky was still dark, but the upper windows of the tall buildings across the Hudson were already reflecting the red morning sun. Glowing windows—he had seen the burning light of the setting sun in the windows of Manhattan skyscrapers. This city isn't just a forest, he thought, it is also mountains, alps.

He had dreamed of Cucuron, of the cats, and of Françoise. In the dream they had packed their suitcases and put them in the car, but he couldn't recall where they were thinking of going. Or were they running away? Something in the dream frightened him. He still felt the fear.

Is that what my life has become? Things happen that I don't understand and I only react to with fear and awkwardness? I have to act, not react. He had often brooded about this over the past few weeks, though he wasn't quite sure what the difference was.

But maybe what truly matters is not acting and changing the world but *interpreting* differently. Georg laughed and put his arms behind his head. That he was being shadowed was the way *they* interpreted it. Why not interpret the whole thing differently, and see the shadowing as a trail that *he* could follow, an opportunity that *he* could use?

He let his thoughts roam. He imagined himself walking through a dark Riverside Park, the redheaded man some fifty yards behind him: Georg comes to a large tree and reacts, no, acts, with lightning speed. He glances back and sees his shadower sauntering along casually. Georg slips behind the thick tree trunk, hears his heart pounding, and then the steps of his shadower coming closer. Suddenly there is silence. Keep on walking! Georg thinks. Keep going! On the street above, a bus rumbles by. He hears the steps again, hears them hesitate, become decisive, then run. It's all a child's game. He trips the redhead, and even as he falls Georg kicks him in the stomach. He kicks him as he lies there: that's for the cats, that's for the attack, that's for all the pain he has endured for Françoise. His first punch breaks the man's nose. The bleeding face utters words in faulty English: *They had heard he was coming to New York and were worried he would . . .*

Would what? Georg didn't know what his imagination should make the redhead say. That was why he wanted to beat it out of him. But if it wasn't a child's game? Georg trips up the running man, the redhead leaps forward, rolls, and jumps back up before Georg can even steady himself. A knife flashes in the man's hand.

Georg tried another scenario. Where could he get a false beard and color for his face and hair? Where could he get a hat and dark glasses? And what could he wear and take with him so that after a few minutes in a men's room he could turn into someone else? There had to be costume rentals and theatrical wardrobes in the Yellow Pages. But what would his shadower think if he saw him go there? Georg imagined putting black shoe polish in his hair, brown color on his face, and a beard he would make from his pubic and chest hair. He peered under the covers—there wasn't a lot there.

He heard Larry leaving the apartment. He got up, looked

through the closets, and found a black hat and a light-colored nylon coat that was rolled up. If he buttoned it up all the way, nothing but the knot of his tie would show. There were a dozen ties hanging on the inside of the closet door. He put everything back in place.

All morning he strolled down Broadway, keeping an eye out for the shadower. The weather had changed. The sky hung low and gray, and the air was warm and humid. The people hurrying by had left their coats and jackets at home, and only the panhandlers were wrapped in layers of clothing, some holding out paper cups in gloved hands begging for money. The storm broke, and Georg took shelter beneath the awning of a fruit stand. Beside him were heaps of melons, pineapples, apples, and peaches. There was a pleasant aroma. He watched the flow of buses, trucks, bright-colored cars, and yellow cabs.

The rain stopped, and he walked on. He went into several drugstores. He found some tan coloring that was good enough in the first one. However, the drugstores didn't sell false beards or the kind of hair dye that could be quickly applied or sprayed on. He looked for his shadower in vain. Between Seventy-eighth and Seventy-ninth streets he almost walked past the Paper House store with its greeting cards for every occasion and masks of Mickey Mouse, King Kong, Dracula, and Frankenstein's monster. Shrink-wrapped beards, side-burns, and mustaches of shiny, black synthetic fiber hung by the entrance. He wanted to get to the greeting-card section in case the shadower peered through the store window. He quickly grabbed one of the beards and found a selection of hairspray in all colors, took a can with a black cap, picked three greeting cards at random, and paid the cashier before anyone stopped outside the store window. He put the beard and the hairspray in his coat pocket and stood by the door, looking at the cards he had bought: "Be My Valentine." Three times.

At the optician's, he quickly hid the sunglasses he had bought in his bag, and stood outside again polishing his own glasses before anyone had a chance to walk by.

He no longer left his apartment without a plastic bag. In it were the hat, the coat, a tie, the brown tanning color, the black hairspray, the beard, and a small mirror. But either no one was shadowing him, or he didn't see anyone. He took the subway to Brooklyn to meet the head of the kindergarten, who, it turned out, couldn't tell him any more about Françoise than the former head of the Ladies Guild in Queens had. Again he stood outside the Polish and Soviet consulates, but every time he walked away he didn't notice anyone shadowing him. Mostly he wandered the streets aimlessly, only occasionally glancing back sheepishly to see if he was being followed. Sometimes he got lost. That didn't worry him—sooner or later he always found a subway station. The weather remained stormy and humid. He now saw the city as a living organism, a hissing dragon, or the kind of gigantic whale that castaways in old adventure books mistook for islands. The whale spouted fountains of water from time to time, and its sweat evaporated in a haze.

One evening Georg went out with Helen. He had given much thought to what he would tell her about himself as they were getting to know each other. He had been a lawyer in Germany and had lived in France as a translator and writer—so far so good. But what was he doing in New York? He told her he was doing research for a book, but then also told her about Françoise, that he had met her in Cucuron, and was looking for her in New York. A lame story, he himself realized. It wasn't surprising that Helen seemed more comfortable talking to the waiter than to him. Her manner struck him as friendly but cautious. They were having dinner at Pertutti, an Italian restaurant on Broadway not far from Columbia. She often went there for lunch. The place reminded him of his own student years, and his lunches and dinners with friends.

He found it hard to talk, not only because he was worried he would reveal too much, but because he was out of practice. In the past he had enjoyed intellectual exchanges: talking about books, movies, politics, and at the same time talking about oneself, mirroring what one had read or seen in one's own experience, and then presenting one's experience in general terms, grasping and analyzing developments and relations of others as prototypes. He could no longer do this. He hadn't done any of this since he had moved from Karlsruhe to Cucuron, and after he had taken over Maurin's translation agency in Marseille, he had barely read a book or seen a movie. With Françoise he had only spoken about everyday matters. When friends had come from Germany, they had talked about what they were doing and about old times. Georg felt foolish next to Helen, who drew parallels between her students and students in general, spoke about the fairy tales she was working on for her dissertation, trends in the German short story, and Germany's turmoil in the nineteenth century; about National Socialism, anti-Semitism, and anti-Americanism; and of her experiences as a student in Trier.

"Did you visit Marx's birthplace in Trier?" he asked.

Helen shook her head. "Have you?"

"No."

"Why bring up Marx?" she asked, relieved that he had said something after his long interlude of nodding and smiling. She reached for her glass and took a sip.

"I've been thinking about something he wrote that has to do with changing and interpreting the world," Georg said, and tried to explain why it was important not to take others' behavior as they mean it, but to determine the meaning oneself.

"Isn't that . . . isn't that what the insane do?" Helen said. "Not caring about what people mean, but seeing in other people's actions what they want to see?"

"What they want to see, or what they are compelled to? If they can choose, then they live with freedom of action instead of having to react. And freedom of action doesn't automatically bring success and happiness. Moreover, when dealing with those whose behavior is so powerful that one can only react, insanity is perhaps better than submission."

She didn't understand him. He didn't understand himself either.

"Is that what you're writing about?" she asked.

He looked at her. "Are you joking?" he said. "We've been sitting here for two hours, and I can't even talk properly about students, books, and politics, and you expect me to write about philosophy or whatever?"

"The problem here seems to be linguistic."

"Fair enough. I'm sorry I asked you out. I've ruined your evening. I didn't realize that I've"—he couldn't find the right expression—"that I've lost so much of my social skills."

The check had been lying on the table for some time. He took some money out of his pocket. She watched him silently, her eyes once again careful. They got up, and he walked with her along Broadway and then up Riverside Drive to where she lived.

"Do you want to come up for a drink?"

They hadn't said a word all the way to her place. In the elevator she asked him what his sign was, and he asked her what hers was. They were both Capricorns. In her apartment, she asked him about Françoise.

"Do you love her?"

"I don't know."

"Why are you avoiding my question?"

"Why are you asking? I mean, why are you asking whether I love her?"

"I'd like to know more about you, so I have to start some-where."

"I don't know a lot about you either."

"That's true."

He looked at her. Her eyes were cautious again. Perhaps her cautiousness has nothing to do with me, he thought, perhaps it's always there. What striking features she has. She's attractive in a sharp sort of way. And still, even with her hair drawn back into a stern ponytail, she looks friendly.

She smiled. "Would you like to see me again?"

"Yes, I would." He was sitting next to her on the couch, and caressed her hand, his fingers running along her veins. "I don't have much money left. Would a walk through Central Park with a Coke and french fries on a park bench be okay?"

She nodded.

"Then I'll be on my way."

"Stay."

He stayed. He woke up often and looked at her as she slept lying on her back in her buttoned-up nightdress, her arms stretched out beside her. The cat was sleeping at his feet. The warmth of the shared bed and the memory of her embraces were pleasant. It was like a homecoming. But always, when he came home, he doubted whether he still belonged there.

27

TWICE THE FOLLOWING DAY GEORG was under the impression that he had seen the same balding man in a gray shirt, light brown pants, and black shoes following him. But he wasn't sure. The day after, Georg was waiting for the bus on Sixth Avenue. It was four o'clock and the street was busy, but it was before rush hour. When the light turned red, there was silence for a few seconds before the traffic came pouring in from the side streets.

He was tired, and only looked up from time to time to see if his bus was coming. He wouldn't have looked across the street if a truck hadn't rammed a cab. And he wouldn't have noticed the redhead, who had been standing behind the truck and now slowly walked on.

Georg looked down the avenue again: there was no sign of a bus. He picked up his plastic bag and started walking. He walked slowly so that the redhead could follow him, but with determination, as was to be expected from someone who has waited long enough for a bus and decided it would be faster to walk. Sixth Avenue, Forty-second Street, Vanderbilt Avenue. The whole way, he didn't look back. If the redhead wasn't following him, too bad. Before going into Grand Central, he dropped a coin and bent down to look for it. People bumped into him and squeezed past. Twenty-one, twenty-two—he counted with clenched teeth. This had to be enough time for the redhead to have seen him. He straightened up and went into the station.

Aha, Georg thought, I see that I can't get away from cathedrals. The high, flat vault, and in front a gigantic photograph of hot-air balloons before liftoff. The broad steps to the left and right leading down from the street to the hall were worthy of a palace, but of a cathedral too. In the middle of the hall was a circular information booth of stone and transparent, dark blue glass with a brass sphere on top that proclaimed the time from four round dials in four directions. It looked almost like a monstrance. Georg walked down the stairs and found his bearings. To his right was the ticket counter, and above it the boards with the arrival and departure times of the trains. It was twenty past four, and at four-forty there was a train bound for Stamford. He bought a ticket for White Plains. Now he could while away the time. He strolled through the main concourse, peering into the passageways leading down to the trains. He read the flickering electronic signs indicating the share prices and currency exchange and the prices for cotton, coffee, and sugar. He went into a smaller hall where there was a newspaper stand, heavy wooden benches, and restroom signs. Five chandeliers hung from the five vaults of the ceiling.

He sat down on a bench and took a newspaper out of his bag. Has he followed me? Is he watching me? While he was strolling through the halls Georg hadn't seen the redhead; he hadn't wanted him to realize he was keeping an eye out for him. Can he watch me discreetly in such a place, or did he see me buying a ticket and is waiting for me to come back into the concourse before my train leaves?

He got up and followed the sign to the men's room—a hallway, a door, a large white room with a long row of urinals and men's backs, and on the other side a long row of white doors. A janitor in white overalls was cleaning the washbasins, humming a song.

It was time for action: close the door, turn the key, pour everything out of the bag onto the floor. Where can I set up my mirror? Will it stay upright on the toilet tank if I lean it against my wallet? He squatted before the mirror, covered his face and neck with a handkerchief, and sprayed black color onto his hair. He rubbed it in, and sprayed again. He wiped away the excess, applied the skin color, stuck on his beard, and tied his tie. He thought he looked like a villain in an old action movie, and once he had put on the dark glasses, like a silent-film-era shyster. The main thing was that he could barely recognize himself. When he got up and put on his coat and hat, he caught sight of his gray sneakers. He blackened them with the rest of the hairspray.

Nobody noticed him when he came out of the stall. He headed to the concourse, trying to walk differently, swaying, with small steps.

The redhead was standing beneath a poster in which Snoopy was advertising MetLife. Georg bought a copy of the *New York Times* and began leafing through it. The redhead was looking around. He walked on, and Georg folded his paper and followed him through the concourse. From the top of the flight of stairs, Georg saw him watching people. The redhead kept looking at the departures board. It wasn't easy: it was rush hour, and a steady stream of people was pouring down the stairs. The redhead gave up. He let the stream carry him, jostled his way out of the concourse while trying to keep a lookout, but the stream carried him through the corridor leading to the subway. Georg followed the crowds down a ramp and a flight of stairs, through the turnstile, and onto the subway platform. The redhead was standing farther up the platform, and Georg made his way toward him. The downtown Lexington Avenue Express arrived, and he managed to get into the same car. So the fellow wasn't heading to the Soviet or the Polish consulate.

They got off at Union Square. They went up the stairs, through the park with the sparse grass and benches that were spotty and leprous and had not been painted in a long time, and onto Broadway, which here was narrow and shabby. The redhead was walking fast. After a couple of blocks, he entered a building.

Georg stopped. It was an old building, with dirty brown brickwork and columns between the windows. Above the ground floor with a shuttered storefront he counted nine floors and half of a tenth, a construction of Roman arches and columns. Above the narrow entrance he read MACINTYRE BUILDING, 874. It towered over the others around it. It had seen better days, but still had a shabby dignity.

The door was locked. There was no way of looking into the hallway where he might see an elevator and an indicator light that would show what floor the redhead was going to. Next to the second buzzer Georg made out *Anderson,* and next to the fifth there was a new bronze plaque with fancy lettering that said TOWNSEND ENTERPRISES. The names next to the other bells were faded or nonexistent.

What was he to do now? It was a quarter past five, the traffic was heavy. He crossed the street and stopped in front of the window of a sports store, keeping an eye on the entrance to the building. At a quarter to six the redhead came out, carrying a briefcase. With him was a young man in jeans and a blue shirt, its top buttons undone. Shortly after six, a group of young women left the building—secretaries, Georg surmised—and toward seven a number of gentlemen in dark suits. It was getting dark, and on the fifth and sixth floors the lights came on.

He was tired. He was sweating beneath the nylon of his coat, his beard itched, and his back ached. With exhaustion came disappointment. Each time the door opened, he had hoped to see Françoise, or at least Bulnakov, or—he himself didn't know who.

Patience is a virtue, as the saying goes. But then again, nobody ever feels the virtue of standing around patiently. We are taught at an early age that you earn your bread by the sweat of your brow, and that we can count on success if we work hard enough at something. What we do not learn is to wait. All of this went through Georg's mind. If only he could wait, knowing that there would be an outcome. But he had no idea whether he had gotten even an inch closer to Françoise.

28

BY SEVEN THE FOLLOWING MORNING GEORG was back at the MacIntyre Building. He had decided against the hairspray, the tanning color, and the coat and hat, and settled for a mustache and sunglasses instead. He walked along the opposite side of the street. From a window table at McDonald's he could keep the entrance in sight, as well as from what he had learned to identify as a classic New York diner on the corner. But since he wanted to be able to see the door buzzers, to see which one the redhead would ring, he had to stand in a doorway across the street. He was eyed suspiciously by everyone coming in, and soon the super appeared to ask what he was doing there. Georg told him his girlfriend worked across the street and that she was coming back from a trip, but that he didn't know exactly at what time. She was going to go straight to work, and he didn't want to miss her. What company was she working for? Georg said he didn't know, otherwise he wouldn't be standing there but would have left her a message. All he knew, Georg said, was that she worked across the street, as he'd picked her up often enough.

"Why don't you just go ask for her across the street?"

The question was so simple and logical that Georg couldn't come up with anything. He crossed the street, the super watching him as he went. He rang the bottom buzzer. He didn't know what he would say if anyone answered, nor did he know why he didn't just pretend to ring the bell, or simply walk away. The intercom remained silent, and he rang the next bell. The super was still watching him. Suddenly the redhead came walking up the street. He was walking fast, his arms swinging. Georg turned around and walked away. It took all his strength to walk calmly. He wanted to run. His heart was pounding. After twenty yards he looked back and saw neither the redhead nor the super.

That evening Helen took him to a baseball game; the Yankees were playing the Cleveland Indians. The stadium looked enormous, even from outside. But after they had taken the escalators, gone up the ramps, and climbed the stairs to their seats, Georg felt as if they were sitting on the rim of a gigantic crater, one side of which had been blown away. The upper tier sloped steeply. Below it a further tier sloped gently down to the playing field. The pitcher, the catcher, the batter, and all the rest of the players Helen pointed out to him were as small as toy figures. There was a flat row of panels and monitors the size of movie screens at the far end of the playing field, and he could see the buildings of the Bronx, and above them the darkening evening sky.

Helen explained the game, and Georg managed to follow it. The pitcher throws the ball to the catcher, and the batter has to try to hit the flying ball with his bat and drive it as far away as possible, while he runs to a certain point before the ball is thrown there and caught by someone. The game keeps stopping, the players change their roles, and balls are thrown and caught by the players in the team as if for practice or fun. The fans root for their team, boo, clap, and howl, but don't become rowdy, don't smash things, or beat people up. Hot dogs, peanuts, and beer are sold. Just like a picnic, Georg thought. He laid an arm around Helen's shoulder, and in the other hand held a paper cup. He felt great.

"Are you enjoying yourself?" she asked with a smile.

At times the ball soared up through the lights in a steep curve, a white sphere against the dark sky. A seagull flew through the lights above the stadium. The screen showed replays and close-ups of the players. The cameras also panned through the audience.

"Where is that?" Georg shouted at Helen.

"Where is what?"

"On the screen! Where are those people sitting?"

He had seen Françoise, he had seen her face. The screen was now showing a family, a laughing fat man wearing a Yankees cap, and two black girls who saw the camera and waved, all within seconds.

"Those are just people here in the stadium." She didn't understand.

"But where in the stadium? Down there, over there? Where are the cameras?"

He jumped up and ran down the stairs. Françoise had to be sitting down below. The camera had shown seats that were almost at the level of the playing field. He tripped, nearly fell, caught himself, kept running. Aisles, handrails, ushers in red caps, blue shirts, and pants—this is where the better seats began. He jumped railings, climbed over the backs of seats of three empty rows, ran left to the next flight of stairs, and continued his descent. He had dodged an usher, but the usher had seen him. There were more stairs; he ran faster down to the next handrail, beneath which the seats were occupied. He wanted to turn left, to the continuation of the stairs, but he saw an usher there. On the right too. So he jumped over the railing where there was a free seat, made his way along the row, over the back of the next free seat, and then again, and down the stairs.

He came to the railing where the upper tier ended. The players and fans were far below. Had Françoise been wearing something red? A blouse? His eyes scanned the rows, saw red everywhere, barely able to tell women and men apart: jackets, sweatshirts, blouses.

"Françoise!" he yelled. People around him had noticed and, amused by his running and shouting, began to chime in, "Françoise! Françoise!"

When the ushers came, Georg followed them without a word. Not a single person in the lower tier had looked up. The ushers were friendly, asked to see his ticket stub, and escorted him back to the upper seats. Helen was waiting for him.

"I'm sorry, but I have to get down there."

"We're in the final inning. Unless there's a miracle, the Indians will lose within the next two minutes."

He wasn't listening. "I'm really sorry, but I really do have to get down there," he said. He walked over to the aisle. She followed him. "Is this about her? Did you see her? Do you love her so much?"

"Do you know how I can get all the way down? Down to the front rows?" He was walking faster, heading down.

"The game's over, it's over! Did you hear me?"

He stopped. The fans were clapping rhythmically, shouting "Yanks! Yanks!" And within seconds people were pouring into the aisles, and over the ramps and stairs.

"But I have to . . ."

"There are forty thousand people here."

"Forty thousand in a stadium is still better than all the millions in New York," he said stubbornly, but could no longer stop to reason with her as the stream of crowds carried them down the stairs and out onto the street. On the way to the subway, and down on the platform, he craned his neck and looked around.

"What would you have done if—" Helen began, "I mean, what would you do if you found her?" They were standing in front of Helen's house, and she was playing with the buttons of his shirt.

He didn't know what to say. He had imagined all sorts of things: a furious eruption, coolly walking out on her, a stormy or a dignified reconciliation.

"Do you want to get back together with her?"

"I . . ." he began, but fell silent.

"There's not much prospect of success when one has to fight so hard for someone. Being back together might at first be heaven on earth. But then, how can she ever repay what you have suffered on her account? Why should she even want to repay it? Did she ask you to suffer?"

Georg looked at her downcast.

"Call me one of these days," she said, kissed his cheek, and left.

Georg bought a beer and sat down on a bench in Riverside Park. He had no idea what to do, what his next step should be. Tomorrow, he told himself, tomorrow I'll make up my mind. Or else things will figure themselves out. Perhaps patience is a virtue also when it comes to decisions. Perhaps things fall into place on their own.

29

THE FOLLOWING DAY GEORG took particular care with his disguise: the brown tanning color, the black hairspray, mustache, sunglasses, jacket, and tie. The previous day the redhead had turned up at a quarter past eight. Georg waited by the sports store. He saw the redhead arriving, crossed the street, and reached the door just as he did. The redhead looked pleasant enough: his face was scarred by acne, but he had clear blue eyes, strong cheekbones, and a broad smile. With his gray suit and buffalo-leather briefcase, he would have blended in at any investment bank or law firm. He looked at Georg blankly, though perhaps with a touch of curiosity, and rang the fourth-floor bell. Georg pressed the eighth-floor bell.

"Another hot day," Georg said.

"Mm."

The door buzzed. The floor of the hallway and the stairs were covered with gray construction paper. The woodwork and banisters had been sanded down, and a first coat of paint had been applied to the walls. Two wood planks were nailed across the missing elevator door.

"They're still working on the elevator," the redhead said. "You've got quite a climb."

"At least I have company halfway."

The construction paper covering the stairs was slippery. Above the third floor there was a new dark gray carpet, the walls were light gray, and the woodwork had been painted Bordeaux red. There was still a smell of fresh paint. On the fourth floor the red-head wished him a nice day and opened a heavy metallic door that bore no inscription. Georg continued climbing the stairs. On the fifth floor was an opaque brown-tinted glass door that read TOWNSEND ENTERPRISES in gold letters, and on the sixth and seventh floors there were again bare metallic doors. The door on the eighth floor stood ajar and he pushed it open.

The floor was unoccupied. Here, too, there was a fresh coat of paint, construction paper on the floor, ladders, and trestle tables. From a corner window he could see Union Square across tarred rooftops, and farther away the Twin Towers. The redhead probably knew that the eighth floor was empty. He might be suspicious.

Georg went down to the fourth floor and rang the bell at Townsend Enterprises. The door swung open with a soft click and he saw a large room, and on the wall an inlaid gold and bronze map of the world. The door fell shut behind him, and from a hall to the left a woman appeared in a pink blouse, a gray suit, with extravagantly pinned-up black hair and ugly pink glasses.

"Can I help you?"

"I was looking for the law firm of Webster, Katz, and Weingarten on the eighth floor. Do you know where they might have moved?"

"We've only been here for two weeks. I don't know anything about previous tenants. Would you like me to check the phone book?"

"That's very kind of you, but thanks all the same." As he turned to leave, he saw her press the city of Lima on the map, at which the door sprang open. He also noticed to her right a spiral staircase in the corridor leading to the floor below.

He called Mr. Epp from a public phone.

"Do you know how I can find out what kind of company Townsend Enterprises is? It's at 874 Broadway?"

"You could ask for a credit report."

"Where?"

"I'll do it for you. Call me back in a few hours."

Two hours later Georg found out that Townsend Enterprises imported rare woods and precious metals, and that it had gone bankrupt six months ago and been taken over.

"Who took it over?"

"The report doesn't say," Mr. Epp replied.

"But where there's a seller there has to be a buyer."

"You're right, but the buyer didn't appear on the credit report."

"What does that mean?"

"It means that the buyer didn't take out a loan to take over the company. If, for instance, you buy an apartment on Central Park South and pay cash, there won't be a credit report on you. That's a bad example, though, because you'd arouse suspicion if you turned up with half a million dollars in cash. Nor is it necessarily a given that the buyer didn't borrow any money: if he has enough assets to cover the credit, then the creditor doesn't care whether he uses the money to buy Townsend or to go to Bermuda on vacation."

"So how can I find the buyer?"

"If he doesn't want to be found by you or someone like you, there's nothing you can do."

"What about the seller?"

"You can try that. Townsend Enterprises belonged to a Mr. Townsend, who lived in Queens. Perhaps he still does. Would you like his address?"

Georg wrote it down. He went to Queens, but didn't get very far. Mr. Townsend said he wouldn't tell him anything. No, he wouldn't let him in. No, he didn't care how important it was. No, he wouldn't talk to him, even if he paid him. Mr. Townsend kept the chain on the door.

Georg called home to Germany, the call costing him more money than he had. But in the end his parents and some friends promised to wire him seven thousand marks.

Then he called Helen. "Can we meet this evening? I have a problem I can't solve. I'd like to discuss it with you." It was a difficult call for him to make.

"All right," she replied hesitantly.

30

THEY MET AGAIN AT PERTUTTI and waited for a table.

"What did you do today?" he asked.

"I spent the day writing."

"What were you writing?"

"My thesis."

"What part are you working on right now?"

"The Brothers Grimm had various versions of their fairy tales, and . . . oh, let's forget about that. You're not really interested, and I'm not either right now. If you aren't ready to start on what you wanted to talk to me about, then don't say anything. That seems to be your specialty."

They remained silent until they were seated at the table, had ordered, and had a bottle of wine in front of them.

"It's about that girl from France, the one I told you about."

"The one you're looking for? You want me to help you find her?"

He rolled the wineglass back and forth between his palms.

"That's what it is, isn't it," she continued. "You sleep with me, but she's the one you want to be with. And now you're asking me to help you get back together with her? Don't you think that's a bit twisted?"

"I'm sorry if I hurt you, Helen. I didn't mean to. The night we spent together was wonderful, and I wasn't thinking about Françoise. You asked if I still love her. I really don't know. But I must find her. I need to know what it was between her and me—whether it was all in my imagination. I don't trust anyone or anything anymore, especially not myself and my feelings. I . . . it's as if everything is blocked and grinding to a halt."

"What is it you imagined?"

"That everything between her and me was perfect. Like with no other woman."

Helen looked at him sadly.

"I can't tell you the whole tangled story," he went on. "I think you'll see why when I tell you what I *can* tell you. If you'd rather I didn't"—he looked up and saw that the waitress had brought their food—"then we can just have our spaghetti." He sprinkled some cheese on his dish. "You told me last night that I need to figure out what I want. I don't just want to find her—I want to put my life back on track. I want to be able to connect with people again, to talk about myself, listen to people, ask for advice when I'm stuck, and even for help. I don't think you took what I said before seriously, but it *is* true, I *have* lost my social skills. I think I'll go crazy if I go on like this." He laughed. "I know I can't expect people to welcome me back with open arms, but I also know I can't go off and feel sorry for myself if they don't." He wound the spaghetti around his fork. "You know, I probably should be happy I could even ask you."

"And what is the question you would be happy to ask if you could ask?"

"Ah, you've happened upon one of those linguistic issues."

"No, it's a logical one. And I didn't happen upon it—I crafted it. But do go on."

He pushed his full plate to the side. "I don't even know what her name is. In France she called herself Françoise Kramsky, but I'm certain that's not her name. The French and Polish background reflected in that name might be real, but then again it might just have been part of the role she was playing. She was passing herself off as a Polish woman who has to work for the Polish or Russian secret service because her parents and brother back in Poland are in danger. For all I know this may or may not be the case. Either way, she used to live in New York, and I think she's still living here. After yesterday, I believe this more than ever."

"How do you know she used to live here?"

Georg told her about the poster in Françoise's room in Cadenet, about his looking for her at the cathedral, and about his meeting with Calvin Cope. "And you saw what happened yesterday evening at the game," he added.

"Are you saying that the only thing you knew when you came to New York was that . . . I mean, all you had to go on was a poster of a cathedral in New York? I used to have a poster on my wall of Gripsholm Castle!"

"But you didn't make a secret of the fact that it *was* Gripsholm Castle. Françoise had cut off the wording at the bottom of the poster and told me it was the church in Warsaw where her parents got married. Be that as it may, I now know that she took part in the theater workshop at the cathedral, and that in any event nobody here seemed to have taken her for Polish or Russian. So she not only speaks French, but also English, and both, it seems, fluently."

"Does she speak Polish too?" Helen asked.

"I don't know. I don't know any Polish."

"She couldn't have known that. She must have anticipated that you might know Polish. Go on."

"I've told you pretty much all I know. I have reason to believe that her previous employer has an office near Union Square, and that she might still be working for him."

"Do you have the address?"

"Yes."

"You went there?"

"I went a couple of times, but didn't see her going in or coming out."

"So you're saying . . . you're saying that the Polish or Russian secret service is operating here in Manhattan? And you know the address? Sixteenth Street, seventh floor, ring three times, KGB sort of thing?"

"No, I'm not saying that. But in Cucuron they threatened me, followed me, and beat me up, and here they've been shadowing me. There's no rhyme or reason for all this, except that it must be the same Polish or Russian secret service. And the fellow who's been following me goes to work every morning and then returns there in the evening after his day of shadowing."

"Your spaghetti's getting cold."

He pulled the plate toward him and began to eat. "It's already cold."

She had finished eating. "So you're asking me how you should go looking for Françoise because I live in New York and might have some ideas about how to find someone in this city. Good, I'll share my ideas with you. But whether you like it or not, I'll also give you a piece of my mind about the story you've just told me. First, if you believe your girlfriend is in the clutches of an Eastern Bloc secret service and that *you* can free her on your own, that's pure nonsense. If she's in anybody's clutches, then the CIA would do a far better job at freeing her. If she isn't going to the CIA herself, then it's because she can't or doesn't want to be freed. Second, you should go to the CIA too. I don't know what your dealings with the KGB are, but you should have seen your face when you told me about how they beat you up. Do you want to hit back at them? Do you want to blackmail them into returning your girl-friend to you? Do you want compensation for being beaten up? I imagine these secret services are never worth the money put into them, but if they couldn't handle someone like you, nobody would invest a cent in them. I've just tied in my third point with my sec-ond one, but that doesn't matter. To go to the CIA, but also to leave things as they are, wouldn't be a bad idea. I like that neigh-borhood, and it gets to me to hear about a KGB office there. My favorite shops are there and a bunch of galleries are not too far away; there's a nice new restaurant I like, and then the KGB moves in? I don't like that! Don't you feel the same way?"

"Look, Helen, these people have finished me off. They used my love, my abilities, destroyed my life in Cucuron, and beat me up. They instigated a car crash that killed a man. They shot my cats."

"They did what?"

Georg told her. "Perhaps that's how they threaten the free world. I don't mean by instigating car crashes and shooting cats, but by manipulating people. In which case my revenge will have something to do with the worldwide battle between good and evil. But that doesn't affect me, and I don't care if they've set up shop near Union Square or Moscow or Cadenet—I don't care a bit. I don't want to let them get away with what they did to me. I want money from them, even if it won't bring back my cats or Maurin, whom I didn't particularly like, but he wasn't a bad guy and never did me any harm. I want money, because they made my life miser-able, and because I don't want to continue living in misery. And also because it will be a defeat for them."

She shrugged her shoulders. "I don't understand you. But, okay: I promised you some ideas. You have that picture of Françoise, right? So I would go to the foreign bookstores, the French and

Polish or Russian ones. I don't know where they are, but I know they exist. I'd also go to libraries with foreign collections. I would go to the restaurants near that office. Above all: since she was in that workshop at the cathedral, she will have lived near here. If she knows French and Polish so well, she will have studied them—probably at Columbia. I'd ask around in the French and Russian departments."

"Do you have any colleagues there?"

"You can give me a picture of her, and I'll ask around." Helen put the picture in her bag, shaking her head. "And when you have your money and your girl—are you going to expose those secret-service people?"

"Expose them? But that would only get them extradited. There was this one guy, Bulnakov, the boss in Cadenet. I would have loved to have strangled him or beaten him to a pulp. I often imagined doing it, but I couldn't bring myself to. If I could have, I wouldn't have been able to live with myself."

"The cats, I keep thinking about your cats. Were they anything like Effi?" She narrowed her eyes, and bit her lips. There was horror and sadness in her face.

"One was white, one was striped, and the third was black with white paws. They were all a year apart, and little Dopey was always putting one over on Sneezy, just like Sneezy had done the year before with Snow White."

"All those names are from *Snow White and the Seven Dwarfs*. What I don't understand: You said that these men destroyed your life in Cucuron. Why did they do it, and how come they managed to do it?"

"I don't know. They must have some link to the French secret service."

"How can the Russian or Polish secret service have a link to the French one? It doesn't make sense."

"Don't ask me. Either way, I didn't get any more translation work, and I had all kinds of trouble with the municipality, the police, the bank, and my landlord."

"What did they figure they'd get out of this?"

"I've asked myself that too. Perhaps they wanted me to be stamped as untrustworthy. Then there wouldn't be anybody I could turn to with my story."

"And you think they also found out about your coming to New York from the French secret service?"

"How else would they have? At any rate, the French customs officer asked me all kinds of questions on my way to Brussels to catch my flight to New York. The French secret service could have found all this out from customs, and the Polish or Russians from them."

"I don't like all this."

Georg still felt that she was convinced he ought to go to the CIA. Was she right? For her the issue didn't seem to be a possible threat to United States', or to European national security. It doesn't matter where the secret service sets up shop—it can do so anywhere. That its work is compromised if people report its activities, if its agents are extradited, and its branches have to move, is of less importance than national security. Georg took Helen's love for the Union Square area seriously. She had a point. Furthermore, he found the idea attractive that a city is a small mirror of the world, containing within it life and work, business and religion, wealth and poverty, black and white, CIA and KGB. That's what he liked about New York: it is the whole world, more so than any middle-class German city could be. He tried to explain this to Helen, but couldn't convince her.

31

GEORG ASKED IN FOREIGN bookstores and libraries whether anyone knew Françoise. He showed her photograph at the cash registers and the counters of diners and stores near the MacIntyre Building. To no avail. He called Helen every evening, and she always came up with some excuse about why she hadn't called him, though she had promised to. She hadn't reached any of her colleagues yet.

He no longer cared whether he was being shadowed or not. On the last day of his reconnaissance in the area around the MacIntyre Building, he went into a diner, and, as he stood waiting for a table, saw the redhead having lunch. The diner was packed, and waiters were rushing past with laden trays, while the owner sat more customers by shouting at them where to sit. The redhead was eating a hamburger, drinking a Coke, and reading a newspaper. Just another regular.

Georg made his way through the diner and sat down at the redhead's table. For an instant the man looked surprised, but then recovered his professional cool. "Don't let me disturb you," Georg said. "I think there's no need for introductions. You might know me better than I know you, but I know you well enough to be able to ask you to pass on a message. There's a gentleman in your—your organization with whom I would like to speak. He was working in France not too long ago; perhaps he's still there, I don't know. He called himself Bulnakov. A short man, stout, sixtyish. Do you know him?"

The redhead didn't say anything, nor did he nod or shake his head.

"I'd like to speak to him. I doubt you have his schedule handy, so have him call me to set up an appointment. Tell him it's important. I don't want to be melodramatic, but tell him too that it wouldn't be a good idea to have me killed. I've written down everything I know, and mailed it out. If my friends don't hear from me, they'll mail the information on to Mermoz, the police, and the newspapers."

"Can I take your order?" the waiter asked.

"Could I have a Coke?"

"Diet?"

"No, regular."

"Have you ever thought of dyeing your hair?" Georg asked, feeling like all three musketeers in one. The redhead ran his fingers through his hair. No, he didn't look pleasant after all. His eyes were too small and his nose too wide. Georg didn't wait for his Coke. He got up.

Outside, he was suddenly gripped by fear. Have I gone crazy? How can I get out of this now? Leave the country? Does he know I didn't mail anything to my friends? Georg looked around, saw an empty cab, and flagged it. He had to get home. The trip took half an hour, and thoughts swirled through his mind. He broke into a sweat. He stared intensely at the streets, the traffic, and the people: the horse-drawn carriage that turned in to Central Park; Columbus on his tall column; the Metropolitan Opera; the movie theaters; the restaurants that had been too pricey for him and of which he made a mental note for better times; the benches on the median strip of Broadway, where he wanted some day to while away an afternoon; the little park on 106th Street, whose grass, trees, and benches had turned gray from the pollution; the ladders hanging from the fire escapes.

He waited for the elevator, his knees shaking. The other day Helen hadn't felt too well, and told him "My legs are like noodles," and he had asked her, "Al dente?" at which she had laughed. The silly scene seemed to him the height of happy normalcy. In his room, he lay down on his bed. He fell asleep and dreamed of Françoise, Bulnakov, and the redhead—he was being shadowed, he ran for all he was worth; then he was sitting on a rock in Central Park, the clouds black and hanging low, but the sun had found a hole and made colors shine. There was utter silence. Georg tugged at a blade of grass, and when it came out of the ground together with a long root, he heard a whimpering that grew louder and louder, until it boomed through the park like a thundering howl. He woke up drenched in sweat. Down in the street a police car had driven by. He heard the siren fade in the distance. He got up and took a shower. His fear was gone. He was ready for action.

32

THE CALL FROM TOWNSEND ENTERPRISES came the following morning at ten.

"Georg! Telephone!" Larry shouted from the kitchen where he was eating breakfast.

"It's a woman, not Helen, though," he whispered to Georg. He and Larry had had dinner with Helen the previous evening. Georg had talked a lot, joked, flirted, and Larry and Helen had looked at him in surprise. What had gotten into this quiet roommate and difficult bedfellow? When Georg took Helen home, they walked past a panhandler, and Helen dropped a coin into his cup. She told Georg how in her first few weeks in New York she had been appalled at all the poverty and had put money in all the cups, until a man called out after her, "Hey, you just threw a quarter in my coffee!" Georg shook with laughter. He got the impression that Helen might have liked to take him upstairs but that she found his sudden cheeriness a little frightening. She still hadn't found anything out about Françoise.

"Mr. Polger? I'm calling from Townsend Enterprises. Mr. Benton would like to know whether you could come by this afternoon. Do you have our address?"

"Please tell Mr. Benton that I'll be there at four."

Georg hung up. He could tell that Larry was curious, but didn't say anything to him. Georg took a cup of coffee to his room, and got a pen and some paper.

> *Dear Jürgen,*
> *I'm sure you'll be surprised at getting a letter from me from*
> *New York. You'll be even more surprised that I am asking*
> *you to open the enclosed envelope only in the event that you*
> *don't hear from me again within four weeks. I know it*
> *sounds a bit cloak-and-dagger, maybe even foolish. It might*
> *even remind you of the games we used to play. And yet, it*
> *might not sound childish to you at all: as the district judge*
> *for Mosbach you must have gotten used to all kinds of*
> *things. Be that as it may, I would be grateful if you did this*
> *for me, and hope to be in contact with you very soon. Give*
> *my best to Anne and the children. Your old friend—*

Then Georg wrote down what he knew, guessed, supposed, and feared, and put the thick batch of papers into an envelope, which he crammed into a second larger envelope, and took it to the post office. He didn't know if he was being watched. But he imagined himself walking to a mailbox, dropping the letter in, walking on, and suddenly hearing a bang, a flame shooting out of the mailbox, with letters fluttering all over Broadway. They wouldn't be able to blow up a whole post office, though.

At four o'clock he was standing outside the MacIntyre Building. The door was open and painters were working in the lobby. The same dark-haired beauty with the ugly glasses let him in, and showed him into a small, windowless conference room. "Mr. Benton will be with you in a moment."

The room was gloomy. Dim light came from a slot between the

low ceiling and the wall. Six chairs of dark leather stood around a heavy table made of dark wood. Set into the wall was an empty black screen. The air conditioner was humming.

Georg looked around for a dimmer to turn up the light. He couldn't find one. There was no knob on the door either. The screen lit up with a gentle buzz, and a small image appeared in the middle and grew, coming toward Georg until it filled the screen. There was a lot of black, with flitting yellow and red lights. It took him a few moments to realize that these were video shots taken from a moving car: yellow headlights and red brake lights that jerked with the rattling of the car from which the video was shot. At times the windshield wipers, the hood, the edge of the windshield, or the steering wheel came into the picture. The car was going fast, and yellow headlights came racing by. It was following another car's red brake lights on the right side of the road and, trailing them, switched to pass the other cars on the left. The passing maneuvers were rough and aggressive, and the approaching headlights shot like a spray of sparks off the screen. The film had no sound. The traffic grew lighter. When there were no more oncoming headlights, and only the red brake lights were ahead, the car swerved next to the other car in front, the camera swinging toward its interior, to the profile of the driver and his hands on the steering wheel. The image kept jumping, showing a trouser leg and the roof of the car, as if the hand holding the camera had been knocked aside. For a few moments Georg couldn't make out anything. Then both cars were in the picture. They had stopped, one having forced the other into a ditch. In the glare of the headlights, Georg could see two men beating up a third. Pummeling him. The third man collapsed, and the two other men began kicking him. The camera zoomed in, showing the bloody head of the man who was lying motionless on the ground. It showed his face from the side, and the tip of a shoe that pushed his head to the other side. It showed his face from the front. The image on the screen disappeared with a light crackle. A chill ran down his spine. That was him. They had made a video of beating him up on the road back from Marseille.

"My young friend!" The door opened, the room brightened, and an effervescent Bulnakov came bursting in. He was just as fat, but now had on a blue three-piece suit. Gone were the shirt with the unbuttoned collar, the rolled-up sleeves, and the patches of sweat under his arms. There was a hint of eau de cologne. His English had the same hard tone as his French. "I can't believe Janis made you wait here in this horrible little room. Come with me into my office."

Georg followed Bulnakov past the map of the world and up the spiral staircase to the next floor, through an empty room with large pictures of trees, and through a double door. Bulnakov was talking incessantly. "This is quite different from my office in Cadenet, isn't it? I'd have preferred a green carpet here. If you ask me, they overdid it a bit with the color of the wood, and without the green of the leaves, there's no brown of the trees. The fight I had to put up for those pictures! Ah, but roughing it over there in the south of France had its charm too. Those were good days! Speaking of south, did you know that New York lies on the same latitude as Rome? You've already had a taste of the heat and humidity here. You just up and came to New York, to the New World! I'll admit I was taken aback! I would never have thought you capable of that! But here you are, and I welcome you to the Big Apple and my office!"

He shut the door. It was a corner room with windows on two sides, a bare wall, and a wall with a picture of two beach chairs beneath an umbrella by the sea. In the corner between the windows stood the large desk, and across from it a sofa and chairs. They sat down. He's all show, Georg thought, and not even especially good at it. The gloomy room they had put him in for the movie, the door without a knob—that had been quite something. But they'd have done better to corner him right then and there: with the walk to Bulnakov's office and all of Bulnakov's swagger, Georg's fear had dissipated.

"One look at you, and I can see you're a changed man," Bulnakov said. "This is no longer the timid young . . ."

"We've been through all that before. I'm sure you know what I want. I don't like Provence anymore, and Provence doesn't like me. Beginning a new life in a new place takes money. And I want that money from you."

Bulnakov sighed. "Money . . . Had you agreed to my proposal back in Cadenet, we could have saved ourselves a whole lot of trouble. Especially you. But let's forget about that, it's water under the bridge, over and done with, *finito*! You see, I have no funds in connection with this matter anymore." He held his empty hands out to Georg.

"Over and done with?" Georg replied. "Surely this story has the kind of plot that could go on. In fact, it *has* gone on quite excitingly for me: scene changes, a world metropolis instead of the back of beyond, this elegant office instead of the little poky one, rare woods and precious gems instead of technical translations, Mr. Benton instead of Monsieur Bulnakov. And yet the interests and the players are still the same. The next episode could be a winner if journalists, the police, and the CIA make an entrance."

"Let's not go into all that again. We already established back in Cadenet that the last thing *you* want is police involvement," Bulnakov said, shaking his head with the kindly but impatient expression usually reserved for a petulant child.

"I came to you because what *I* want is two million dollars. I'd be happier with those two million than having to deal with the police, the CIA, or reporters, but if I don't get the money, I'm quite prepared to endure the little bit of trouble the police might put me through." Georg stressed *little bit* and *trouble*.

"Two million dollars? Are you mad?"

"Fine, then let's make it three. You mustn't forget that I'm quite irritated. I loved my life in Cucuron, my cats, and my physical well-being. I'd need a large sum of money to turn my back on all the fuss I could make."

Bulnakov laughed. "How do you picture your next step? You just go waltzing over to the CIA, ask for whoever's on duty, and tell him your story? Whisper in his ear that Townsend Enterprises is a front for . . ."

" . . . the Polish or even the Russian secret service."

"And they'll lap it all up, no questions asked? I have to say . . ." Bulnakov continued laughing, slapping his thighs, his belly hopping.

Georg waited. "In case you're interested," he began, and Bulnakov fell silent, "First of all I'd go to the press and show them all my papers and photographs. I'd let them decide when I should go to the CIA or the police. They'll have their own ideas about timing and so on. Furthermore . . . as I've just seen in your screening room, you have quite a bit of photographic material yourself, but still you might like this little souvenir of the good times, our good times, back in Provence." Georg took out the photograph of Bulnakov sitting behind the wheel of his Lancia, his arm resting on the rolled-down window, the sun in his face and on the license plate. He reached across the table and handed it to him.

"It's a nice picture," Bulnakov said. "And how nicely you put it: 'the good times in Provence.' It *is* amazing how you've developed. What a pity that you weren't then who you are now. I'm sorry to bring this up again, but we could have worked so well together. As for the money . . ." He shook his head. "Even if we forget your little joke about the three million, I can't see how . . . not to mention . . ." He rested his head on his right hand, and with his middle finger rubbed his left eyebrow. Then he sat up. "Give me a few days. I need to give this some thought and make a few calls. Can we reach you at your friend's number?"

At the door Georg asked about Françoise. "Is she okay?"

"Most definitely. She's living a quieter life, doesn't get out much. She'll go to a baseball game now and then," Bulnakov said with a smile. "You might even bump into her at one. I hear you've become a Yankees fan."

33

THE NEXT FEW DAYS were like a vacation for Georg. He spent them in Riverside Park. A blanket of heat was smothering the streets, but in the park there was a breeze from the river. He even put up with the pigeons. They covered the benches with their droppings and nodded their heads idiotically. Sparrows bathed in the dust. Squirrels darted nervously across the paths. The same homeless people sat on the same benches at the same time every day. The same joggers jogged. The same people walked the same dogs, some picking up the dog shit with plastic bags, others letting it lie, looking around guiltily. The same little brats in designer T-shirts terrorized the same black nannies.

Georg was pleased with the way his meeting with Bulnakov had gone. He hadn't expected him to agree to his demand for money, let alone that he'd have paid it right away. Georg was happy to make Bulnakov squirm for a while before he would grudgingly realize that he had no other choice.

One afternoon there was a sudden thunderstorm, but Georg stayed on his park bench. The wind tore through the trees. Rain-drops fell like sparkling pearls in the lightning flashes. Only one of the buildings on the street had a slanting roof, and the water came pouring down the incline, flooding the gutter and spraying over the edge. He was soaked to the skin and very happy.

Sometimes he brought along a book, newspaper, or magazine. It had been a while since he had given any thought to the world at large. Was the world giving any thought to him? He was glad to loosen up a little, now that the world was taking on a friendlier face, and that substantial investments were on the horizon.

There was an article in *Newsweek* that he found particularly interesting. A consortium of European aircraft builders was developing a new attack helicopter, in partnership with the Gorgefield Aircraft Company. A major political breakthrough was in the works: by the late 1990s all the NATO armies were to adopt this single make of attack helicopter. The aim was to break the superiority of the Russians. The conventional wars of the future would be won or lost with attack helicopters. Uniformity in this weapon system was of vital importance, which was why the NATO defense ministers were meeting in Ottawa with a view to clinching this political breakthrough. The technological breakthrough was already under wraps. The article mentioned stub wings, ABC rotors, and RAM-coating.

How very interesting, Georg thought. I'm not surprised that the Russians would do anything to get their hands on Mermoz's plans. Back at the apartment, he took out the copies he had made during his last few weeks of working for Mermoz. He had translated words like *screws, bolts, connectors, valves, spindles, flanges, nuts, clamps, caps, joints, spars, flex beams, mufflers, regulators, filters, slots, axels, rotors,* and so on, without being interested in what they meant. Now he tried to decode their meaning.

In a nearby bookstore he found a book about attack helicopters and read up on stub wings, ABC rotors, and RAM-coating. Stub wings help support the rotor and carry the weapons. As Georg read on, he realized that the suspensions were connected to the stub wings. He also recognized that on his plans the rotors were closely stacked over one another, which in the ABC concept had the advancing blades providing more thrust than the retrograde blades, giving the helicopter the remarkable speed of over three hundred miles per hour. Finally he thought he had decoded the last series of plans. There were slots at the rear letting out compressed air, helping to make the tail rotor redundant. Sensational. He didn't have the plans for the radar absorbing RAM-coating, but here it seemed to be more of a problem of the material and pricing than one of construction. About the Hokum, the newest Soviet attack helicopter, the book did not have much to say. But if it was true that the Hokum still used a tail rotor and could only reach speeds of two hundred miles per hour, then the Soviets had every reason to be alarmed by the NATO developments.

On Sunday he went to pick up Helen to take her out to brunch. The money from Germany had arrived. He had paid the rent, and had a thick roll of hundred-dollar bills hidden in his belt, and a wad of twenties in his pocket. He felt rich. Helen should enjoy his good times. When he arrived she was on the phone.

"No, Max, both shoulders. Take hold of both shoulders with both hands and fold them back until they meet. Now take both shoulders in one hand. Are you holding them? No, Max, not the sleeves. . . . Of course I know that the sleeves begin at the shoulders, and if you mean the beginning of the sleeves . . . Are you holding both shoulders where the sleeves begin with one hand? Good, then with the other, fold the side with the buttons . . . over the other side . . . the side with the buttonholes. You can't? . . . Because you're holding both shoulders together with your hand? You've got to let go for a second. Then you can fold the side with the buttons over the side with the buttonholes, so that only the lining is visible. What? The jacket fell on the floor? You let go of it? You can only let go of it once you've folded one side over the other. . . . You can't?" She got up, cradled the phone between her ear and shoulder, and took her jacket off the back of a chair. "You see, Max, I know what I'm talking about. I worked in a clothing store. I have a jacket in my hands right now. . . ." She folded it as she had described. You learn something every day, Georg thought. "I know you can't see me. 'You see' is just a turn of phrase. Of course I know you can't see me. All I wanted to say was, I have a jacket in my hands right now and it's quite simple when the hand that holds both shoulders from inside . . . no, Max, I'm not coming over to pack your jackets for you. No. You don't have many jackets, just one? Then why don't you just wear it? Because it's too warm in Italy? Listen, Max, I've got to go. Call me this evening. . . . Keep practicing. Or don't take the jacket with you, if it'll be too hot for you anyway. . . ." Helen had spoken the whole time with the utmost seriousness. Now she threw Georg an impatient, exasperated look. "Listen, I really have to go. Yes, I'm hanging up. Yes, now."

She hung up and looked at Georg. "That was Max."

"I heard."

"He wanted me to tell him how to fold a jacket in order to pack it into a suitcase."

"How does one do that? Does one take both shoulders in . . ."

"Stop making fun of me. Shall we go?"

He flagged down a cab on Broadway. Helen was surprised. They took a table in the garden at Julia's, an elegant restaurant on Seventy-ninth Street, and ordered eggs Benedict and Bloody Marys.

"I thought you said our next date would be a walk in the park, with french fries and a Coke?"

"Things have changed."

"Is the KGB footing the bill?" she asked, with a touch of irony.

"Don't worry, this is honest money we're squandering here. I got money from Germany."

"Have you given any thought to going to the CIA or the FBI?"

She was getting on his nerves. "To be honest, no. Is the cross-examination over?"

"Well," she said hesitantly, "if you didn't want my opinion, you shouldn't have told me anything. Now it's too late. I thought about all this, and the more I thought about it, the less I understand you. Unless you're cynical."

"What?"

"Cynical. I mean . . . in my definition, cynicism is contempt for everything that holds our world together: solidarity, order, responsibility. I'm not saying that law and order should reign supreme. But you Germans don't understand that. When I was an exchange student in Krefeld, I saw how in class you all copy one another. No sign of a bad conscience, as if it were the noblest deed." She shook her head.

"But if the students are all copying one another, then that's surely a prime example of solidarity," Georg said.

"Solidarity in the face of order imposed from above. For you guys, order is still imposed from above, and either you worship it or you try, like naughty children, to bamboozle it."

He laughed. "Perhaps you're right, but that's not being cynical, not in your definition either. Contempt is missing."

"You think it's funny, but it isn't a laughing matter. Contempt comes later, when the children have grown up." The eggs Benedict arrived. "Do you understand what I'm saying?" Helen insisted.

"I've got to think about it for a moment," he replied.

He savored every bite. As he relaxed, he thought the matter over. He wasn't sure if Helen was right or not, but it was true that he didn't care about solidarity, order, and responsibility. He didn't think of himself as immoral. One didn't trample on the weak, exploit the poor, or cheat the simpleminded. But that had nothing to do with solidarity, order, and responsibility. It was a question of instinct, and reached only so far as one can perceive the consequences of one's actions. There were certain things one simply didn't do, because one wouldn't be able to face oneself in the mirror. One doesn't like to face oneself in the mirror when one has pimples either, but one's complexion is not a question of morals. Could it be that I'm not immoral but amoral? Can I tell Helen that?

"What you're saying would mean that we have still not left our authoritarian state behind us," he said. "You have a point there. It's like what you told me the other day about the fairy tales in the nineteenth century, which I wanted to ask you a few more questions about—"

"You want to drop the matter," she cut in. "Fine, I'm dropping it. What shall we do after brunch? Can I have another Bloody Mary?"

They left Julia's and strolled through Central Park to the Metropolitan Museum. A new annex had been built, and one could step out onto the roof. They stood above the trees in the park. Like on a jetty above a green lake of swaying treetops surrounded by a mountain range of buildings.

34

GEORG WAS ALWAYS SURPRISED by the speed with which construction jobs were carried out in New York, work that in France or Germany would have taken days or weeks to complete. One Saturday morning he was awakened by the noise of construction machinery breaking up the sidewalk the whole length of 115th Street. By evening the new pavement was ready, light gray cement divided into large squares, and the soil around the trees was framed by dark red bricks. Farther down Broadway he saw a building of forty or fifty stories going up. The first time he had gone past there were only cranes towering into the sky, then steel went up, and now the skeleton of the building had turned into a massive body. But at Townsend Enterprises things were not moving ahead. On Monday morning Georg was awakened by a phone call telling him to be at the office by ten, and as he climbed the stairs, the painters were still at work.

He waited in front of the map of the world, and was greeted coolly by Bulnakov who didn't show him to his office, but to a room with two metal desks, a metal filing cabinet, and far too many metal chairs. There were open drawers, yellowing papers on the floor, the water in the cooler was brackish and brown, and there was dust everywhere. Bulnakov leaned against the window while Georg stood in the middle of the room.

"I am happy to be able to make you an offer, Mr. Polger," Bulnakov said. "We can offer you thirty thousand dollars and a guarantee that the problems you faced in Cucuron will not recur. We will also provide you with a ticket back to Marseille or Brussels, whichever you prefer. That will be the end of the matter, and the end of your stay in the New World. This evening you will take TWA flight 126 or Air France flight 212. Bookings have been made for you on both planes. All I need is your signature, here." Bulnakov's hand slipped into his left inside jacket pocket and took out a thick wad of bills, laid them on the desk, and from his right outer pocket took a folded piece of paper that he handed to Georg.

Sometimes it seems as if the world holds its breath for an instant. It is as if all the wheels stand still, all the airplanes, tennis balls, and swallows hang in the air, as if all movement were frozen. It is as if the earth were hesitating, uncertain whether to keep turning forward, turn back, or change the axis around which it rotates. The stillness is absolute. Traffic falls silent, no machine rumbles, no wave slaps the shore, no wind rustles through the leaves. At such a moment everything seems possible: the movements of the world are made up of infinitely small states of motionlessness, and one can imagine these states gathering together in a different order of things.

This happens often at moments when decisions must be made. The beloved is still standing in the door of the railway car and you can still say "stay" before the conductor blows his whistle, the door falls shut, and the train pulls out of the station. Or it is you who is standing in the door of the railway car waiting for her to say "stay." The world can hold its breath as much in moments of another person's decision as it can for one's own. Even if it is not a matter of a momentous decision: when one sits in a café drinking a cup of cocoa, watching passersby through the window, when one stops for a moment while doing the ironing, or when one has just screwed on the nib of a fountain pen. It is a matter of course that the way of the world could be different.

But it's not a matter of course either. Georg saw the frozen movement of Bulnakov's outstretched hand, saw the piece of paper, didn't hear the traffic or the footsteps in the hall outside. Thirty thousand dollars—sixty thousand marks, a hundred and eighty thousand francs. That was more than he needed to live a year in Cucuron. Hadn't he always wanted time and leisure to write? Wasn't he tired of crossing swords with Bulnakov and searching for Françoise? But even as these thoughts flashed through his mind, he knew that there was nothing to think about or decide.

"Thanks but no thanks, Monsieur Bulnakov."

Bulnakov went to the door, opened it, and called in two men. They wore gray suits and had policemen's faces. "Take Mr. Polger to the airport," Bulnakov said to them, "and see to it that he gets on the plane to Brussels or Marseille, as we have arranged. He can have his luggage sent on after him." He stuck the wad of bills back in his pocket and left the room. As far as he was concerned, Georg no longer existed.

Georg hesitated, but one of the men reached for his arm. *Come along,* his expression said, *or I'll break all your bones.* Georg decided to walk ahead, and the two men followed him. The beautiful dark-haired woman at the reception buzzed them out.

In the stairwell, one of the men stayed at Georg's side, the other followed behind. Georg set the pace. Damn! he thought. Damn! On the third-floor landing he saw the open elevator shaft with the wood planks nailed across the missing door, and on the way down to the second floor heard the painters working below. It was worth a try.

Before they reached the second-floor landing, he stopped and bent down as if to tie his shoelace. The man behind him stopped too, while the one beside him continued walking the few steps down to the landing, where he turned back with an expectant look. He had been descending the stairs on Georg's right, along the wall, and now stood in front of the wood planks across the open elevator shaft. Georg untied his shoelace and then tied it again. He got up and took a step forward. The man on the landing turned away and waited for Georg to come down. Georg lunged forward and rammed his shoulder and arm into the man's back with all the force he could muster. He heard splintering wood and a surprised cry, followed by a shout of horror. Georg didn't look back, he just ran, made it down the first flight, past the bend in the stairwell, another flight of stairs, tripped on the paper the painters had put down to protect the floor of the landing, caught himself, and saw the startled faces of the painters, who were too taken aback to try to stop him. Behind him he heard the other man's loud and heavy steps. The painters were crowded to the right along the wall, and on the left were the cans of paint by the banister. Georg kicked over a large bucket of paint blocking the way, jumped over as it tumbled, and took three steps in one stride. He reached the last bend in the stairwell, the last flight of stairs, when he heard a crash. This time he quickly turned around. The man following him had slipped on the paint and came sliding down the stairs on his back, his head banging against the steps as he went, and finally crashed into the wall. Georg bounded down the last few stairs, ran through the hall, out the door, and into the street.

He kept running, weaving through a throng of pedestrians and dodging cars to get to the other side of the street. He looked back: nobody was following him. He hailed a cab and headed home. Larry wasn't there.

He stood in his room and looked in the mirror. His face,

though unchanged, looked alien to him. Did I kill that man? He realized that his whole body was drenched in sweat. He took a shower. A towel around his middle, he was pouring himself some coffee in the kitchen when the doorbell rang. He tiptoed across the hall and looked through the peephole: two men of the same type as the ones who were to escort him to the airport. They rang again, and exchanged a few hushed words that Georg couldn't catch. One of them leaned against the wall across the landing, while the other disappeared from Georg's field of vision. Georg waited. The man by the wall changed his position from time to time. Georg thought about how by now he could have been on his way to the airport with thirty thousand dollars in his pocket. Or had they just wanted to get him out of the building and into a car so they could kill him somewhere along the way? What did these two bastards out there want from him? Should he wait for Larry, and leave the building with him? Where would he go? As it was, he had to wait for Larry and ask him for the name of that *New York Times* reporter he had met at his party. Why hadn't I asked him before?

Georg got dressed and put everything he wanted to show the reporter into a folder: the copies of the Mermoz plans, the photographs he had taken of Bulnakov and his men in Pertuis, the newspaper article, the helicopter book, the photograph of Françoise. Through the peephole he saw Larry with a Food Market bag in one hand and his key in the other. One of the bastards was talking up a storm, and Larry was shaking his head and shrugging his shoulders. He turned to the door, and put the key in the lock. His face was near and large in the peephole, his mouth and nose distorted, his eyes, hair, and chin receding grotesquely.

Georg had reached the kitchen window before the door even opened, pulled the kitchen window guard open, and swung himself out onto the fire escape. With a tug he pulled the guard shut again, and with a few jumps found himself in front of the kitchen window on the floor below. The fire escape vibrated and rattled, the echo clanging against the walls of the narrow courtyard. He cowered beneath the windowsill and waited for the echo to die away. He listened for a sound from above: nothing. He looked down: trash cans, trash bags, a cat.

He waited twenty minutes. Should I have stayed upstairs to help Larry in case those bastards attacked him? But perhaps things have turned out for the best because I wasn't there. If one of them had burst into the apartment with Larry, seen me, thrown himself at me, and Larry had tried to stop him—perhaps the guy would have drawn a revolver, or pistol, or whatever they're called. He imagined the scene. He wondered what to do next. He couldn't go back to Larry's apartment anymore. To Helen's? There would probably be men there too, and furthermore he didn't want to put her in harm's way.

He was still holding the folder with the material for the press. I must find that reporter, he told himself. Then he, the CIA, or the FBI will take charge. But what can they do? What will happen if Bulnakov and his people go underground, disappear, cover their tracks, or if the material I've gathered isn't substantial enough? Then at least I can pack my things in peace and fly back home. *Home?*

But there would be time enough to think about all that later. Now he had to see how he would get through the rest of the day and the night. He knew that Larry was planning to go to Long Island to see a literary critic, and that he was thinking of spending the night there. Her name was Mary. Larry said she was a beautiful woman, this literary critic, or critical literate, or literally critical. Larry had mentioned her full name, but Georg couldn't remember it, so wouldn't be able to reach him there. He looked at his watch. It wasn't even noon yet.

He carefully climbed down the fire escape, trying not to make any noise or startle housewives at their kitchen windows. On the third floor, the window and the window guard were open. The kitchen was empty, there were no pots on the stove, no dishes in the sink, no open box of cornflakes or newspaper lying on the table. He climbed through the window and walked through the rooms. The blinds were down, their slats throwing light and shade onto the freshly painted walls and polished floors. The apartment was waiting to be lived in again. Georg carefully put the chain on the door. He wanted to hear in time if the super or the new tenants showed up. He lay down on the floor near the front door.

35

WHEN HE WOKE UP it was dark outside. His body was aching from the hard floor. He got up, walked around the apartment, and looked outside. He gazed into lit windows. The streetlights were on, and 115th Street was quiet. On Broadway, the headlights of cars flitted past. It was eleven o'clock. He had slept deeply. He was hungry.

He couldn't think clearly yet. He climbed down the fire escape to the courtyard, reached the cellar, stole past the laundry room and the super's office, and found the door from which steps led up to the sidewalk by the main entrance. Only after he had pulled the door shut behind him did he realize that he wouldn't be able to get back in again, and that he should have tried to return to Larry's apartment. Spending the night on an empty stomach in an empty apartment was still better than spending it . . . spending it where? He had no idea where to go.

He waited a long time to make sure that nobody suspicious was standing in one of the doorways, under an awning, or behind a parked car. He didn't see anyone. He decided not to go down Broadway, but went to Riverside Drive and walked in the shadow of the park to where it ended at Seventy-second Street. He crossed

West End Avenue and Broadway, and went into an Italian restaurant on Columbus. It was expensive, but the service was fast and the pasta was good. Georg had washed his face in the men's room, combed his hair, and been pleased with what he saw in the mirror. He enjoyed his meal. He had survived. After a whole bottle of Cabernet Sauvignon, he was convinced he had won. He chuckled at the thought of those two bastards from Bulnakov's office, the splintering wood, the shout from the elevator shaft, and the man who tripped over the bucket of paint and fell down the stairs. I did all that, he thought triumphantly. Too bad I couldn't stop and watch. The two of them must really have been a sight.

He spent the night on a park bench, his head resting on the folder for the reporter. Other people lay on park benches too. He didn't stand out in his sneakers, jeans, polo shirt, and his old blue jacket. He woke up from time to time, heard dogs barking, drunks quarreling, a siren howling. He turned over and fell asleep again. In the morning there was a slight chill in the air, and he curled up. At six o'clock he went to a diner and had some eggs and bacon with home fries, toast and jelly, and coffee. His head was heavy from the wine. He was sure he could reach Larry later in the morning. He rehearsed mentally what he would tell the reporter, how he would show him the plans and photos, how he would explain it all. He found a copy of the *Times* next to him on the counter, abandoned by its owner, and read about Afghanistan and Nicaragua, a promising Democratic presidential candidate, and the trade deficit.

In the Metro section he read: "Two officers were injured yesterday while attempting to arrest and deport an illegal alien. One officer is still at the FDR Hospital, the other was released after treatment of minor injuries. The foreigner, a German by the name of Georg Polger, is now a fugitive. Anyone with information . . ."

At first Georg's mind was a blank. Then the same thoughts kept recurring: This doesn't make sense, it doesn't make sense at all. The Russians might have some plants in the French secret service, but surely not in the American one. And even if they did have plants here, then surely not to the extent that they could send officers out after him.

Georg went through what he knew one step at a time, as he had arranged the information for the reporter. A European consortium— Britain, Germany, Italy, and France—come together to develop a new attack helicopter. Is that clear enough so far? Yes. They achieve a technological breakthrough. It's not about a faster helicopter with stronger armor and higher payload: it's about a war machine that can annihilate all other weapon systems. Consequently, the helicopter is scheduled for adoption not only by the four European countries that created it but by all the NATO countries, including the United States. That's clear enough too. It is also clear that the Russians are interested in getting in on the act. They contacted him in the guise of the translation agency and saw to it that *he* became the head of a translation agency that worked almost exclusively for Mermoz, and then got at the plans through *him*. Still clear? Yes, still clear.

But Georg had difficulty piecing together how the story went on. He remembered Helen's asking why the Russians or the Poles would want to destroy his life in Cucuron, and how they had managed it. He, and Helen too, had taken it for granted that they would want to sideline him as a source, to make him untrustworthy, and that consequently they had given the French damning evidence implicating him. But why did they bother with that when they could simply retreat behind the iron curtain, which was still ironclad enough to stop anyone from investigating further? Georg was aware, however, that the Russians found knowledge far more valuable when others didn't know they had it. The question remained how they had compromised Georg with the French, and how they had made him seem untrustworthy, making his life in

Cucuron miserable. There were endless possibilities. So far so good? Something was bothering Georg: he was no longer pleased with the way the story went on, but didn't know what it was that was bothering him, or what other scenarios might be possible.

Now to New York and Townsend Enterprises. To sum up, he had hit upon the idea of New York because of the poster in Françoise's room, he had looked for her here, and had made certain people nervous. Then he was shadowed, and had shadowed the redhead, and had found Townsend Enterprises. So much was clear, because that is what had actually happened. The rest was unclear: why would the KGB send people from New York, of all places, to Provence? In the case of Bulnakov, that might still make sense. Georg thought of Philip Habib who had been sent by the Americans on difficult missions throughout the world, and of Hans-Jürgen Wischnewski who had been sent out by the Germans. But to send Françoise on an international mission? The KGB had agents in New York. Their front is disguised as an enterprise specializing in rare woods and precious metals. Why woods and metals of all things? Enough's enough, Georg told himself, who cares whether they deal in woods, metals, flowers, or books? Bulnakov, the chief agent, is sent on a particularly important mission to France because he is a very experienced agent. He takes Françoise, a fellow agent, with him because she is his mistress. Can one KGB agent be the lover of another? Georg sighed. Whether or not the KGB allowed its agents to climb into bed with one another, it would not have officers of the CIA, the FBI, or the New York Police Department working for it.

He ordered another cup of coffee. Regardless of how the officers became involved, they were after him now. Did they still just want to deport him? Or drag him before a court? Or deport him and make sure he ended up before a German court? I could see a lawyer, Georg thought, or, better, I could go find that reporter and then talk to a lawyer.

The newspaper was still lying in front of him. The title photo showed the aircraft carrier *Tennessee* entering the Gulf of Mexico, with two helicopters hovering above it. Georg's glance rested on the two helicopters, moved away, and then returned to them.

Two helicopters, he thought, not one. He had read in the *Newsweek* article that in the development of a new attack helicopter for the NATO armies, a consortium of European aircraft builders was developing a new attack helicopter in competition with Gorgefield, an American company based in California. Both parties were proposing a similar helicopter with stub wings, ABC rotors, and RAM-coating. Both parties, it was rumored, had made the same technological breakthrough.

Georg couldn't remember whether this concerned the wings, the rotors, or the coating, but he remembered clearly that it was the same breakthrough: the helicopters had the same qualities and performance capabilities.

So this is not about the Soviets and the Europeans, but about Gorgefield and Mermoz! Had Bulnakov come up with a double disguise: as an Eastern Bloc agent and the head of a translation agency? As he went through the story again Georg considered his questions—the important as well as the less important ones. Bulnakov was less important. Important was who he worked for. The CIA? Georg could imagine the worst of any secret service, but he couldn't imagine the CIA undertaking industrial espionage, espionage at a European industrial enterprise working under contract to an American one. That the CIA might cover and help with such espionage was possible, and would explain the two agents in the MacIntyre Building. It would also explain the attitude of the French. Bulnakov would have asked the CIA to put in a word with the French secret service, which would have passed the information he wanted to disseminate about Georg to the police, the town council, the bank, and Georg's landlord.

But if Bulnakov wasn't working for the CIA, who was he work-ing for? And what about Townsend Enterprises? Was it Gorgefield Aircraft's own secret service, its department specializing in sensitive issues, dirty business? Or was Bulnakov, or Benton, as Georg was beginning to call him, an independent contractor whose company, Townsend Enterprises, could be hired to carry out shady deals ranging from espionage to murder? Had Gorgefield hired Townsend Enterprises for Operation Mermoz? They had probably given the job a more elegant name: the Mermoz Study, the Mer-moz Investigation, the European Helicopter Project.

Even without being able to answer these questions, the story now made sense. Françoise was from New York, worked for Townsend Enterprises in New York, had worked in Cadenet, and then returned to New York. Was she still working for Townsend? Was she still Bulnakov's/Benton's lover?

Georg had a story that made sense, but no idea what to do next. He didn't know if he could interest a reporter in it, or if news-papers would print such a story or readers would want to read it. As it was, he didn't have much evidence, and didn't see how he could get more. Without evidence a lawyer couldn't help him either—that is, if a lawyer would even want to help him. The authorities are looking for me, damn it! I'm a wanted man!

Should he give up or go on? Those were the two alternatives he had been considering. Now he didn't even know what they meant. What should he go on doing, and how? Did giving up mean going to the police, to the German consulate, going underground in the city, or going out West? Georg paid and left. If nothing else, he could at least fill in the gaps of the story. The library at Columbia must have technical journals dealing with helicopters, weapon sys-tems, and the armaments industry that could clarify whether Gorgefield Aircraft had put out the concept of its helicopter after Operation Mermoz. It could also clarify whether Townsend Enterprises was a branch of Gorgefield or an independent company that belonged to Benton. Georg wanted to know, even if he wasn't sure how this knowledge could help him.

He called Helen from a pay phone. "It's me, Georg."

"You're calling in the middle of the night? . . . Oh, it's seven. God, is everything all right?"

"I'm sorry, it's again about the matter I told you about. . . ."

"I tried calling you yesterday evening. A year ago your girl-friend"—she said the word as coolly as she could—"was living on Prince Street. A colleague of mine in the Russian Department had her in her conversation class."

"Where?"

"In her conversation class . . . Oh, 160 Prince Street near Sixth Avenue and Houston."

Georg took a deep breath. "Thank you, Helen. I hope this didn't . . ."

"No, it didn't put me out. I showed my colleague the picture, and she gave me her address. And her name: Fran Kramer."

"Fran Kramer . . . I looked for Kramers in the phone book. You wouldn't believe how many there are. Kramers, Krameks, Kram-erovs, and so on. Three whole pages."

"Mm."

"Anyway, thanks. Would you be mad at me if I asked for one more favor?"

"If I was, you wouldn't ask?"

"Since the CIA is already mad at me, or the FBI, or the police, I don't know who, I'd be happier if you weren't too."

"What are you talking about?"

Georg told her. He had gone over the story so many times in his mind, in true and false versions, that he managed to tell her in a few words. "And as a result," he concluded, "you'll find me in today's *New York Times,* on page fourteen."

"What are you going to do?"

"I don't know. I have no idea what they're intending to do to me, how intensively they're looking for me, or who's looking. Can you call Townsend Enterprises and act like you are an executive secretary calling from IBM, Nabisco, or Mercedes-Benz, and tell them you would like to make an appointment for someone to discuss an important security issue? If they fall for it, then it would point to the fact that Townsend is an independent enterprise, rather than a branch of Gorgefield Aircraft."

"Don't you have more immediate problems?"

"I do, but this one I believe we can get to the bottom of. I want to know what's going on at Townsend. Not to mention that it would be a relief to know I'm not up against America's most important armaments enterprise, but that crazy cowboy Benton."

"But isn't it clear already that Gorgefield Aircraft . . . I mean, could Benton send government officers to do his dirty work?"

"Who knows? Would you do me the favor and call? Call from a quiet pay phone somewhere, and the matter can be dealt with in two or three minutes."

"Okay, I'll give it a try later this morning. This evening you can reach me at home. In the afternoon I'll be at Columbia. Be careful."

36

AT THE ENTRANCE OF the Seventy-ninth Street subway station Georg was about to rush down the stairs with the throng of people when he realized the absurdity of hurrying. The one thing he had more than enough of was time. He would walk.

He strolled up Amsterdam Avenue toward Columbia. He didn't think the library would be open before eight. He remembered that he had walked up Amsterdam once before, on his first day in New York, from the Epps' apartment to the cathedral. That had been two months ago. Back then nobody was out to get him, he knew where he would sleep, and he could return to Germany at any time. Nothing was left of that now. And yet he felt lighthearted. The first few weeks in New York he had been stumbling around in the dark. He had felt as if a wound was being relentlessly rubbed raw. He had arrived in America wounded, and every pointless movement had hurt and exhausted him, driven him further into the wariness and distrust he had brought with him from Cucuron. Bulnakov/Benton was right: he had become another person.

The cathedral loomed gray and heavy in the morning sun. Water was bubbling out of the fountain beside it, tables were being set up on the sidewalk in front of the Hungarian Pastry Shop, and workmen were laying pipes in the middle of the street. It was a pleasantly familiar scene, and because of that familiarity Georg let down his guard. Initially, he had intended to enter the Columbia campus from the back gate on Amsterdam Avenue, though he had no reason to think they would expect him to turn up at Columbia, and hence lie in wait for him. So he decided to head for the main gate, which was closer, and he turned onto 114th Street. Not because of the three minutes he would save. It just seemed to make more sense.

They must have been standing on the corner of Broadway, keeping an eye on the subway entrance; God knows why. Perhaps they'd been waiting on the corner of 115th Street by Larry's apartment, and had gone for a stroll to stretch their legs. Georg saw the redhead and turned around, but the redhead had seen him and began to run toward him, as did the man who was with him.

Georg ran back down 114th Street to Amsterdam. The other two were fast catching up. He turned to look, and was alarmed at how close they were getting. He wouldn't be able to keep up this speed. If he could get to the cathedral before the others did he had a chance! If it was already open, if the others didn't know about the little side entrance, if the side entrance was open. If not—he didn't have the time to think about that. He sprinted across the street, cars honking their horns and braking. His heart was pounding, his legs weren't as fast as he wanted them to be. Before the others managed to cross the street, he had reached the steps in front of the cathedral leading up to an array of doors that were always locked and one door that he hoped to God was open. He raced up the steps two at a time, his legs getting weaker. He pushed against the door. It didn't move. He pushed harder, rattled it, the door moved, and, as he pulled, it swung open heavily. He looked back over his shoulder—the others had crossed the street and reached the bottom of the stairs. Would they try the wrong door? He ran through the nave. He kept looking back, hoping his footsteps wouldn't give him away. The columns blocked his view of the doors, and he walked slowly. The interior of the cathedral was warm. The air was musty and heavy. It was quiet, the church was empty. From the ceiling hung a large fish made of pipes which from the tail to the head grew in length and then became shorter again, bright colors shining as the pipes trembled in the cathedral's draft. Far behind him he heard a door slamming shut.

He had reached the side door before the others saw him. It wasn't locked and he slipped out, closing it silently behind him. Again he ran: through the yard, the garden, across Amsterdam Avenue, along 110th Street to Broadway, and down into the subway station.

He hadn't seen the redhead or the other man come out of the cathedral, and hadn't seen them when he'd looked back on Broadway. Down in the subway he kept his eyes on the stairs until the train arrived, and kept looking at the platform from the subway car until the doors slid shut and the train jolted into motion.

He sat down, leaned his head against the window, and closed his eyes. He felt a pain in his chest, and his legs were heavy and tired. Those men meant business. They were out to get him. Where else might they be looking for him? In hotels? Did they have pictures of him? Was his picture now flickering on every monitor in every police station?

The train rolled from station to station. People got on and off. He would have loved to sit like this forever, fall asleep, and wake up in another time and place.

Part Three

37

GEORG GOT OFF THE SUBWAY. The stairs leading up to the street stank of piss. Trucks roared along Houston Street, and the air they churned up made shreds of paper and newspaper pages flutter like tired birds over the dusty median strip. In the distance he could make out green fire escapes fronting red brick facades, which looked like urban hanging gardens.

On the right he looked down quiet, well-tended streets. Behind a church dedicated to Saint Anthony of Padua, whose Romanesque style reminded him of the Wilhelmine style of his high-school gym, he turned onto Thompson Street. Again, well-preserved four- and five-story buildings, on the ground floor shops selling antiques, art, or fashion. Above the buildings at the end of the street the towers of the World Trade Center seemed near enough to touch. At the next intersection Georg was on Prince Street.

Only by looking closely could he read above the entrance of the building on the corner, in faded gold lettering, 160 PRINCE. Café Borgia II was just opening for business across the street. He sat by the window and ordered an orange juice. He studied the building on the corner as if he would have to sketch it from memory one day. Red brick, high windows, decorative gables whose gray stone rose up like crowns, forming little temple friezes on the top story. Beside the entrance, there was the Vesuvio Bakery on one side and on the other a bar whose window advertised Miller beer in swooping, red-neon writing. The building had five stories. Between the second and third a band of gray stone looped around the building. There were black fire escapes, and a hydrant in front of the entrance.

The café was empty. The radio was playing oldies. On the street a Vesuvio Bakery delivery truck drove up. A mail truck came, stopped, and drove on.

Even before he could make out Françoise's face he recognized her walk, the bouncy swing of her skirt and hips, the small quick steps of her short legs. She was pushing a shopping cart; sometimes she gave it a forward push, letting it roll, then catching up with it. She was laughing. No, it wasn't a shopping cart, it was a stroller; out of which two tiny arms reached up.

In front of the entrance she carefully lifted up the baby. When Georg was fifteen, and for the first time unhappy in love, at school one afternoon he saw his sweetheart from a landing. She was down in the hall, leaning on the railing, cuddling a kitten from the litter of the janitor's cat. Nevertheless, jealousy tore through him so painfully, so physically, in a way he had never experienced since. Now he saw Françoise holding the baby on her arm and wrapping it in a blanket, and for a moment jealousy convulsed his body and reminded him of the scene with the kitten.

With her foot and free hand Françoise folded the stroller and went into the building. Rage built up in Georg, a cold, bright desire to strike out, hurt, destroy. He paid and went across the street. *Fran Kramer, fifth floor, apartment 5B.* The outer door was open. He went up the stairs. Bicycles, strollers, tied bundles of cardboard, and garbage cans stood on the landings. The folded stroller was leaning beside the door to 5B. He rang.

"Coming!"

He heard her move a chair, come to the door, put on the security chain, and unlock the door. The child was screaming. The door opened a crack. He saw the chain and Françoise's frightened, familiar, and forlorn face.

With a kick he broke the chain and pushed the door open. She recoiled, pressed herself against the wall, covering her breast with her hands. He was struck by the stains on her blouse and her oily hair; he had never seen her other than well-groomed and stylish.

"You?"

"Yes, me!" He stepped into the small vestibule and shut the door.

"But how . . . what . . . what are you doing here?" She looked at him horrified.

"What am I doing here in your apartment?"

"In my apartment, in the city . . . where have you been? How did you know?"

"That you lived here?" he asked.

"How did you find out? . . ."

"You mean to tell me you didn't know I was in town? You of all people?" He shook his head. "The child is crying."

Steadying herself against the wall, she made her way to the living room. "I'm sorry. . . . I was just . . ." She went over to the baby, who was lying on a blanket on the floor waving its arms and legs, and picked it up. Her blouse fell open and he saw her breasts. She sat down on the sofa and put the dripping breast into the crying mouth. The child closed its eyes and sucked. Françoise looked up. No longer upset, no longer afraid. She pushed her lower lip out a little. He knew that gesture. She knew she looked coquettish and sulky like that. In her eyes was the plea for him not to be angry at her, the certainty that he couldn't be angry.

His anger burst out again. "I'm going to stay here for a while, and if you tell Bulnakov or Benton or the CIA or the police . . . if you mention anything to anybody, I'll kill the child. Whose is it? Are you married?" He hadn't even considered this possibility. He glanced around the living room and through the open door at the bedroom, looking for signs that a man was living here.

"I was."

"In Warsaw?" he asked, with a scornful laugh.

"No," she answered seriously, "here in New York. We've just divorced."

"Bulnakov?"

"Nonsense. Benton's my boss, not my husband."

"And whose child is it?"

"No . . . yes . . . well, whose do you think?"

"For heaven's sake, Françoise, can't you say anything besides no and yes?"

"And can you stop cross-examining me in this terrible, revolting way? You come bursting through the door, break my lock, upset Jill, and me as well. I don't want to hear any more!" She said that in her little girl's voice, whimpering and tearful.

"I'll beat it out of you, Françoise, word for word if I have to! Or I'll hang the child up by her feet until you tell me everything I want to know. Who is the father?"

"You are—you won't harm her, right?"

"I don't want to hear any of your nonsense! Who is the father?"

"My ex. Are you satisfied?"

He felt his old helplessness return. He knew he could not hurt her or the baby, but he doubted that she would tell him the truth even then. He would only hear what she thought he wanted to hear in order to get the painful situation over with. She was a child who lived in hope of immediate reward and in fear of immediate punishment. She had no sense of the importance of the truth.

"Don't look at me like that," she said.

"How am I looking at you?"

"Critically . . . no, judgmentally."

He shrugged his shoulders.

"I didn't know . . . didn't want things to happen the way they did," she said. "It lasted much longer than I thought it would, and it was so wonderful to be with you. Do you remember what we were listening to when we were driving to Lyon? A potpourri of music."

"I do," he said. How he remembered the trip, and the night, and the other nights, and waking up beside Françoise, and coming home every evening to Cucuron. The memories were about to seize him and bear him away like a wave. Sentimentality was the last thing he needed.

"Let's talk about that some other time," he said. "I slept last night on a bench in the park, this morning I was chased by Benton's people, and I'm dog-tired. Since Jill is asleep, put her in the crib in the bedroom and I'll sleep there in your bed. I'm going to lock the door from the inside. I know Benton's men can break the door down, but don't forget that I'll be right next to your child, and can get at her before anyone comes bursting in."

"But what if she starts crying?"

"Then I'll wake up and let you in."

"But I don't understand. . . ."

She looked at him helplessly, and he noticed again the little dimple above her right eyebrow.

"You don't need to understand," he said. "Just behave as if

nothing happened, forget you saw me today, forget that I'm here, and see to it that no one finds out!"

She remained seated. He took the baby from her arms, laid it in the crib, and pushed the crib into the bedroom. He locked the door, undressed, and lay down to sleep. He smelled Françoise. From the adjoining room he heard her weeping softly.

38

HE WOKE UP AROUND TWO. There was a gentle knocking. He got up and looked at Jill—she was sleeping with her thumb in her mouth.

"What is it?" he whispered at the door.

"Will you open up?"

He thought for a moment. Was it a trap? If it was, and the child in his power didn't offer him any protection, then he had no chance anyway. He pulled on his jeans and opened the door.

She was wearing the dress she had worn on the trip to Lyon, the pale blue- and red-striped dress with the big blue flowers. She had washed her hair, put on makeup, and was holding a baby bottle in her hand.

"I think Jill will wake up in about an hour," she whispered. "Will you give her her bottle? When you're finished, hold her upright on your shoulder and gently tap her on the back until she burps. And if she's wet, you'll have to go get a fresh diaper. They're in the bathroom."

"Where are you going?"

"I have to deliver some translations."

"You're no longer working for Bulnakov?"

"Yes, I am, but I'm still on maternity leave. I'm translating as a sideline—New York is expensive, you know."

"Were you at the Yankees-Indians game last week?"

"It wasn't much of a game. Did you see it? Now I have to go. Thanks for babysitting." From the apartment door she waved to him, that coquettish fluttering of her hand.

He lay down again. He couldn't sleep anymore, and listened to Jill's satisfied cooing and gurgling. Then he took a shower and shaved with the pink ladies' razor he found on the edge of the bathtub. Under the sink he found some detergent, soaked his underwear, shirt, and socks, and put on his jeans and the biggest sweater he could find in Françoise's closet. When he went over to Jill's crib, she was lying with her eyes open. She looked up at him, screwed up her mouth, and began screaming until she turned red. He lifted her up, forgot where Françoise had put the bottle, and ran through the apartment looking for it. Jill wouldn't stop screaming.

He had never wanted to have children. He had also never wanted not to. The subject had just never interested him. When he and Steffi had gotten married, it was understood that one day they would have children. And with Hanne, who had had herself sterilized, having children was not an option. He had a godson, the oldest son of his school friend Jürgen, who had become a judge in Mosbach, married at twenty-three, and had had five children. Georg had taken his godson to the Frankfurt Zoo and the Mannheim Observatory, had read him bedtime stories whenever he visited, and for his tenth birthday had given him a big Swiss army knife with all its blades, screwdrivers, bottle openers, corkscrews, scissors, file, saw, magnifier, tweezers, toothpick, and a tool to scale fish. Georg would have liked to have had a knife like that himself. It was too heavy for the practical boy, who wasn't the least bit interested in fishing.

Georg found the bottle. Jill emptied it in a flash and went on screaming. What does the brat want now? he wondered. He remembered the instruction to hold her upright and tap her lightly on the back; he did so, she burped, and continued screaming.

"What more do you want? Why are you screaming at me at the top of your lungs? Men don't like women who scream, and they don't like ugly women, and if you go on like this your face will get crooked and you'll be ugly."

Jill quieted down. But as soon as he stopped talking she began screaming again, so he talked and talked, rocked her back and forth, walked her up and down. He couldn't bring himself to utter "oochy-coochy-coo" or "patti-patti-poo," though he realized she'd be just as pleased with those as with any fairy tales, Wild West stories, or detective stories he could remember.

He put her down on the cabinet in the bathroom and removed her wet diaper. It wasn't only full of pee, but full of poop too. He washed her bottom and rubbed lotion on it. He waved Jill's legs in a cycling motion, moved her arms left and right, up and down, and let her hands reach for his thumbs and hold them tight. He pinched the fat on her thighs, arms, and hips. She squealed with delight. Actually, there's almost no difference between little children and little kittens, he thought. Children are more work—one invests more in them, and that's why people later have more to offer than cats have. But that's as it should be. He studied her face, looking for some sign of comprehension. She had thin dark hair, a high forehead, a snub nose and snub chin, and no teeth. He couldn't make out what was going on in her blue eyes; when he bent over her, he saw his reflection in them. She laughed. Was that a sign of comprehension? On the edge of her ears he discovered a thick dark down. She was still holding on to his thumbs.

"My little hostage. No more flirting when Mama comes home. She mustn't find out what a paper tiger I am. Is that clear?"

Jill fell asleep. Georg laid her in her crib, called Jürgen in Germany, and asked him to disregard the letter he hadn't yet gotten. He had decided to replace the old story with the new one, so Jürgen shouldn't bother with the instructions he had enclosed. "But why? And what are you doing in New York?" His friend was concerned.

"I'll call again," Georg said. "Say hi to the kids."

Georg knew there were problems that had to be dealt with and decisions to be made. What should his next step be? What were the others planning? What can I do? he wondered. What do I want to do? But the outside world was far away. He knew the feeling from being in a train: the only things that separated you from the passing landscape, cities, cars, and people were a thin wall and thin glass. But this separation and the speed were enough to encapsulate you. And also, you could no longer do anything where you started from, or at the place you were to arrive. When you got there you might deal with problems and decisions—but in your capsule you were condemned to passivity, and you were free. Also, when no one knows that you are sitting in the train, when no one is expecting you and you are traveling to a completely unknown city, being cut off takes on an existential quality. No car trip can compare with it; as a driver you are busy steering, or as a passenger you are involved in what the driver is doing. In Françoise's apartment Georg was experiencing the same isolation from the world. Of course, all he had to do was walk out and involve himself with the life outside. He knew that that was what he faced, that he had to do it and would. He didn't feel inwardly blocked. It was just that the train hadn't yet arrived, and the schedule with the arrival time had been lost.

He sat in the rocking chair in the living room and looked out the window. An inner courtyard with a tree, fire escapes, clotheslines, and garbage cans. He couldn't distinguish from which apartments the noises came: hammering, the clatter of pots and pans, a saxophone, children's voices, and women chatting loudly across the courtyard. Françoise didn't return. The shadows climbed up the walls. Around six Jill woke up, this time without screaming. When she fell asleep again he rinsed his clothes and hung them up to dry. Twilight was coming on. The sky over the neighboring houses and the World Trade Center turned red.

Françoise came home carrying a large brown shopping bag. "How's Jill?"

"She's asleep."

"Still? She usually wakes up around six."

"She did. I made some tea for her and gave it to her in her bottle."

She looked at him skeptically. "I'm sorry I'm so late. I had to drop by Benton's."

"So you really . . . Where are they? How much time do I have to come out with my hands raised?" He stood up.

"No!" she called out. The shopping bag fell and burst open as she threw herself in front of the door to the bedroom. "Don't do anything to her, don't! I didn't say anything about you! There's an article about you in the *Times,* wait, I'll show it to you." She thrust out her left hand at him as if she were fending him off, bent down, pulled the newspaper from the ruins of the shopping bag, and began leafing through it. "I found it. Here."

"I know the article." So she really believed he was capable of doing something to Jill.

She straightened up. "Next week my vacation is over, and in any case I wanted to go to Townsend, and after reading the article . . ."

"Did you speak to Benton?"

"Yes, he's pretty annoyed. He didn't want that article in the paper. The painters in the stairwell called an ambulance and the police; then the reporters came, nosed around, and the man you pushed down the stairs gave them your name. After he came to, he didn't know what he was doing. It's turned into a circus, Joe said, a regular circus."

"Joe is Benton?"

"Yes. Do you know that the other one, the one who fell into the elevator shaft, broke both his legs?"

"How should I know that? I didn't have time to stop and look."

"Why did you do it?" she asked anxiously. He had become strange to her. Someone who lashes out indiscriminately, and before whom she had better watch her step.

"What did he tell you? Bulnakov—Benton—Joe; soon I'll be calling the bastard sweetie and honey."

"He said you're no longer satisfied with the money you got in Cucuron, that you want more and are trying to blackmail him."

"And what would I blackmail him with?"

"You found out that we . . . that he . . . that you weren't dealing with the Russians in Provence, and you threatened to tell the Russians, and they'd be angry."

"He says I came to him with this idiotic blackmail? And what was I supposed to have got from him in Cucuron?" Georg was really angry. "How stupid do you think I am? You know yourself that it's bullshit—what's this song and dance about? God, I'm fed up with your lies, fed up, fed up!" And with every *fed up* he gave her a slap in the face. He clenched his fists. She shielded herself with her arm. They stood opposite each other. Eye to eye, her terrified look and his enraged one. He took a deep breath. "It's over, I won't do anything more to you. Does Benton come here sometimes? Are you still having an affair with him?"

"That's over. Anyone who comes here calls me up ahead of time in case the child's asleep. You needn't worry. And I certainly haven't breathed a word to anyone. I don't want to lose my babysitter, either." She looked and sounded different from one minute to the next. At first fearful, then conspiratorially serious, and with her last words cheerful, with a wink. "Oh look at this mess!" she said, picking up the burst bag. Milk was leaking onto the floor. "Will you help me with supper?"

Later, when they went to bed, he was unyielding. He took the bed next to Jill, while Françoise slept in the living room on the couch. He locked the door; he would hear Jill if she woke up, and if he didn't, Françoise could knock and wake him up. He did hear Jill when she woke up in the night, even before Françoise did, and went into the other room and woke Françoise up. She gave Jill her breast, and he fell asleep. She took off her nightgown and slipped beside him under the blanket.

39

ALREADY BY THE NEXT DAY living together had become oddly routine. It reminded Georg of their last days together in Cucuron.

"What were you thinking, when from one day to the next you didn't come back? Without a word?" Georg saw the pale blue morning sky through the venetian blind. Françoise lay exhausted and satisfied beside him, her head on his arm.

"Joe sent me to New York and told me to stay here."

"But what were you thinking, I mean about me, about us?"

The strain of her concentrating was visible. She didn't understand his question, but wanted to do the right thing: not disappoint him, but satisfy him with the proper answer.

"Don't think so much," he said. "Just tell me what happened."

"It was my job. And Jill was on the way, and you were beginning to act crazy. I couldn't risk my job, because I soon would have to provide for Jill and couldn't rely on you anymore. You've always been . . . you always want more, and keep doing things that ruin what you have. In Provence, at any rate, you ruined everything with your pride and stubbornness. You just had to quarrel with Joe. In life you have to be content with what you've got."

"That's ridiculous."

"You see? You don't understand."

"Aren't you getting any support for Jill?"

"No, I don't know who the father is."

"Benton or your ex . . . Might she be mine?"

She raised herself on her elbow and looked down at him.

"That's sweet. Sometimes I wished it. How you were in my mind when I was walking along Madison Avenue and a man ran in front of me who was wearing your aftershave, and I ached with longing."

"And later, when Benton came back to New York, he told you that he had finally got the better of me, bought me out?"

"Yes."

"Do you want to know what really happened?"

"Not now. Jill will be waking up in a minute." She pushed the blanket away and kissed his chest.

Georg spent most of the day alone with Jill. Fran, as he now called her, was finishing her new translation at NYU. He called Helen, who had been given an appointment at Townsend Enterprises. He played with Jill, fed and bathed her. He read around in Fran's books and systematically went through her closets, the boxes under her bed, and her desk. He found out that she was thirty years old, came from Baltimore, had gone to Williams College and Columbia, and had been married for six years to a David Kramer. In a drawer he found a photo of himself; he was lying in the hammock in front of the house in Cucuron, with Dopey on his stomach. When Fran came home at six, dinner was on the table.

The following days passed the same way. Evenings and mornings, when they had slept together and Fran was purring with satisfaction, Georg got occasional answers to occasional questions. She had hung up the picture of the cathedral in Cucuron because when she had been a student, she had lived across the street from the cathedral and had been happy and wanted something to remember New York by. Yes, Townsend Enterprises was owned by Joe Benton. He had gotten around in the world, first as an Orthodox priest, then with the U.S. Marines, and then in an ashram in California. When he became a private detective, at first he had worked under his own name. But as his commissions got riskier and his clientele more well known, he had to assume disguises. Fran had worked for him for four years, and had become his lover in the second year. The commission for Gorgefield Aircraft was the biggest she could remember; it brought Joe thirty million. She was sorry it had cost Maurin his life, she said. But Georg had the impression that she didn't care, and that she was somehow making him responsible for the attack on him and the death of his cats. Joe had connections to official authorities. "One hand washes the other, you know. Sometimes he needs the officials, and sometimes they're happy to have a problem disposed of unofficially. CIA? No idea whether it's the CIA or one of its offshoots."

Politics didn't interest Fran. So she wasn't interested in the political dimension of her work, let alone the moral dimension. But, Georg asked himself, am I any different? I told Helen that for Benton/Bulnakov it would mean a defeat to pay me money, and that this defeat was what mattered to me. But what did I want to do with the money? Punish and avenge myself and cash in—I made it pretty easy for myself.

Nevertheless, the question remained what really interested Fran. Her job? She seemed to have an obsequious relation to her work; the obsequious relation to Benton had been part of it. "Did you love him?"—"He wasn't bad to me. I have a lot to thank him for, he even wanted to pay for Jill."—"Why didn't you let him?" Georg wanted to hear her answer. Her submissiveness reminded him of the fatalism with which one submits to the weather, come rain or shine. So she could have taken Benton's money as a gift from heaven. But no. "I can't do that, because I don't know whether he's the father." She seemed surprised at his strange question, morally surprised. So the theory about the weather was out. Still, the job for her was just a job, just like the weather is only the weather; it left her uninvolved.

Jill? Fran's life revolved around Jill. At the same time, Georg saw that in dealing with Jill she was strangely businesslike; Jill was a practical problem requiring practical solutions. When Fran breast-fed her it was a technical procedure of providing and receiving nourishment. There was no mother-child intimacy. Georg recalled paintings in museums that radiated more warmth than the sight of Jill at Fran's breast.

And me? Is she interested in me? Does she love me? Georg often had the feeling that for her he too was a piece of the world that one can't change, that one had to accept, happy when he was happy, and bending under his blows. Every day she was happier with him. He noticed it. And why not? He took care of Jill, cleaned up and cooked for Fran, and slept with her. When she had her orgasm, when cries burst from her and she held on to him tightly—Now, he thought, now I've gotten through to you, shaken you. But when afterward she stretched out, she reminded him of a dog eagerly splashing through water and shaking itself dry, the drops spraying all around. He had not gotten through to her, shaken her, but was simply one of the pleasures the world offered.

Sometimes he wanted to grab and shake her. As if there were another Fran in the Fran he was with, as if he could break through the shell in which she, whether happy or sad, seemed uninvolved and unreachable: to hack his way through the hedge of roses and shake the sleeping princess awake if he couldn't kiss her awake. He knew the feeling from Cucuron. Once, leafing through Helen's books, he had come across the fairy tale of *Sleeping Beauty*. He knew that the king's son who kissed the sleeping princess awake had simply come at the right time. The hundred years had passed, and the day had come when she was to awaken again. Sleeping Beauty is not to be awakened simply by a kiss.

Once Georg did grab Fran and shake her. It was on a Sunday, and for the first time she hadn't gone to the library to translate, but spent the whole day with him. They took Jill into their bed, and the three of them bathed in the bathtub. They had Bloody Marys and eggs Benedict for breakfast, and read their way through the thick Sunday *Times*. At two, the phone rang. Fran picked up, said "yes" and "fine" and "till then." At three she began saying that Sunday together was lovely, but she wasn't used to their being together so much. She needed her space, and time to be alone. He agreed, and went on reading. She asked him whether he didn't feel that way too, and whether he wouldn't like to go out for a few hours.

"In this weather?" He shivered.

"It's just a little rain. It'll be like a blanket, you won't be seen or recognized. You've been cooped up in the apartment all week."

"Maybe later."

At three-thirty she got to the point. "Somebody's coming at four, and I'd be happy if you could leave me alone with him for a while."

"Who's coming? What's going on?"

"Sometimes . . . a man comes to see me and we . . ."

"You sleep together."

She nodded.

"Is he the one who called up before?"

"He's married, and only knows at short notice when he can get away."

"Then he calls up, comes over, you fuck, and he buttons up his pants and leaves."

She didn't say anything.

"Do you love him?"

"No. It's . . . he is . . ."

"Benton?"

She looked at him, afraid. How he knew and hated that glance. And the small, shrill voice in which she finally asked him: "You're not going to do anything to me? Or to Jill?"

The old feeling of helplessness and fatigue came over him. No, he thought, I won't put up with that anymore, but I won't beat her either. "Fran, I don't want this. I'm not sure what our relationship is, but everything will be ruined if you sleep with Benton now, and I don't want everything to be ruined. Don't open the door when he comes." Should he tell her he loved her?

But she had already started rationalizing, sentence after sentence, in a whining voice. "No, Georg, that's impossible. He knows I'm here and that if I'm here I'll open the door. He's coming all the way from Queens. He's my boss, and Monday I've got to go back to work—Monday, that's tomorrow. I won't let you mess up my life. You'd like that, wouldn't you! And how do you imagine it? Joe is outside the door, hears Jill screaming and me running around, and I don't open it? Have you thought of that? It doesn't work that way. You come bursting into my life and make demands. I never promised you anything. And what do you think Joe is going to do when he's outside and I don't let him in? Do you think he'll shrug his shoulders, go down the stairs, get in his car, and go home? He would obviously think something happened to me when I tell him he can come over and then don't open the door. He'll call the super and the fire department, and I wouldn't like to think what would happen then. I . . ."

He grabbed her, shook her, and screamed into her face in which her voiceless mouth went on forming sentences: "Shut up, Fran, stop!" She screwed up her face. "You'll write a note saying you had to take Jill to the hospital, and you'll leave it on the door downstairs. And if he comes up anyway—I'll deal with him, which is perhaps the right end for this crazy story! I've had it!" Jill had woken up and was screaming, and Georg saw the fear again in Fran's look. "Do it, otherwise you and Jill will regret it."

She wrote the note and stuck it on the door downstairs. Benton didn't buzz. They finished reading the paper, cooked together, and went to bed early, because Fran had to be up early. They made love, and it seemed to Georg that she was so passionate because he was so remote.

In his thoughts he was with Townsend Enterprises, Gorgefield Aircraft, and the Russians. He wanted to bring the story to an end. The way the players were placed and the cards dealt, it looked bad for him. The cards needed to be called in, reshuffled, and dealt again—and why not bring in a new player? If the Russians weren't in the game, he'd have to bring them in.

40

IF THE THIRTY MILLION JOE had gotten from Gorgefield Aircraft wasn't enough, and Joe wanted another thirty million from the Russians—how would he go about it? He would make contact, present them with a model construction sketch, and name a price. Joe wouldn't do this as head of Townsend Enterprises—in fact, he would perhaps go through a straw man. How would the Russians react? They would study the designs thoroughly, want details about all the material, haggle over the price, find out whom they were dealing with, and whether they were being taken for a ride. And how would he, Georg, set his trap?

By the time Fran came home from work Monday evening, he had a plan. Up till then, he had celebrated Fran's return home according to the image of the ideal American housewife he had gotten from the movies, with Jill on his arm, dinner on the stove, cocktails in the fridge, and candles on the table. It was an ironic game, but an affectionate one. On this evening, Georg was playing another game.

"Which do you want to hear first, the good news or the bad?" he asked.

Fran realized that something was up, and smiled uncertainly. "The good news."

"I'm leaving in a few days."

"But you have to . . . I mean, we . . ."

He waited, but she couldn't finish the sentence. She looked at him; the dimple above her right eyebrow was trembling. He was hoping that she would . . . he himself didn't know what he was hoping.

"And the bad news?"

"Either you and Jill go with me, or I'll take Jill alone."

"Go where?" There was alarm in her voice.

"To San Francisco, for a week."

"Are you crazy? I started work today and can't take another week off."

"Then I'll go alone with Jill."

She put down the brown shopping bag and put her hands on her hips. "You really are crazy. You and Jill . . . What are you up to? What do you hope to gain from it?"

"I'm taking Jill as a hostage if you really want to know. As a hostage so that you won't say a word to anyone until I come back and get away for good. So you don't run to Joe Benton and betray me."

"I would never do that. I haven't done it all the time you've been here."

"I'm taking her as a hostage so you don't confess to Benton that you copied the Mermoz documents and gave them to me. For that's exactly what you'll do tomorrow or the day after."

"Oh no! I don't know what game you're playing, but it won't work. Even if I wanted to—I just can't, I have no idea where he keeps the documents, how I could get hold of them, how I should copy them—"

"You can photograph them. You know how to do that. And

don't try telling me you can't. . . . You've been his lover for years, you still sleep with him, you know he got thirty million from Gorgefield Aircraft, which you couldn't have learned from the assets report of Townsend Enterprises, you know he arranged Maurin's murder and . . ."

"And your cats, don't forget your cats," she said. He looked at her, dumbfounded. She again had her shrill little girl's voice, but at the same time scorn and sheer hatred in her voice and her narrowed eyes. "You on your high horse! You think you're better than him and better than me. You look down on us. But that's just the way life is, everyone fights for their own piece of the cake, you too, only not as well! Joe didn't make the rules!"

"You don't understand the key point," he said calmly. "All these years you've known Benton well enough to be able to find out where he keeps the Mermoz documents and how you can get hold of them. The point isn't who made the rules. Okay, Benton didn't make them, you didn't make them, I didn't make them. But the thing is that I've finally understood them, just the way you and Benton have long understood them! I have Jill. You get hold of the Mermoz documents. You'll also get hold of the names of Benton's contact at Gorgefield Aircraft and a letterhead of Gorgefield's, a brochure, whatever has the firm's logo on it. If you want Jill back, you'd better get to it."

"You really mean it!"

"Yes, Fran, I really mean it."

"And how do you imagine you and Jill managing in San Francisco?"

"What's to imagine? There must be thousands of fathers on the road with their little daughters. Once I'm there, I'll take her along with me if I can't get a babysitter, and I'll feed her and change her diapers."

"Just like that?"

"Just like that. If you have any advice, I'm all ears. I could buy one of those baby carriers and sling it across my chest—you know the ones I mean."

They looked at each other. In her glance there was no longer hate, only sadness. Sadness? Georg had seen her frightened, anxious, remote, rejecting, hostile, cheerful, but never sad. If she can look like that, he thought, then she really is Sleeping Beauty behind the hedge of roses. Whether she could gaze happily with the same seriousness and collectedness . . . Could she? Now her glance pierced though him—Georg would gladly have asked her what she was thinking. Then there was a bright gurgling in her throat, a smothered laugh that she covered with her hand—perhaps she was amused, imagining Georg with Jill in a sling across his chest. But just for a moment.

"If you really do do that, Georg, I'll never forgive you! Never! To take Jill from me, use her to blackmail me—I can't find words for how despicable I think that is, how low, how cowardly! You haven't been able to fight like a . . . like a man for your piece of the cake, or perhaps you tried and missed out, and now you want to try in some kind of backhanded way, after the fact. . . . What you didn't destroy back then in Cucuron you're destroying now. I know I never should have let myself in for the job in Cucuron, and I ought not to have let it happen between us, or for it to get serious and go on for so long. It was a mistake. I always knew it, but somehow . . . was it the sex? But never mind. Don't destroy everything now. Stay here or leave the country—I'll talk to Joe, and see to it that you can leave without any problems and go back to Cucuron. But don't take Jill away from me and force me to break into Joe's safe like a thief!"

"No, Fran. I'm going to bring this to an end. You think it's already at an end. But it isn't, not for me."

Late in the evening she tried once again to change his mind. She tried the next day and the day after. She tried being calm, then with tears and shouting, with reasoning, pleas, threats, swearing, and seduction. Sometimes he noticed with both shock and relief how afraid of him she was, in the same way she was afraid of Benton.

The next day she brought him the letterhead from Gorgefield Aircraft and the name of Benton's contact there. The day after she brought the cans with the negatives of the construction drawings. On the copies Georg had, the Mermoz logo was barely visible in the lower right corner, where the original had a majestic double-decker plane stamped with the letters *M, E, R, M, O,* and *Z* between the upper and lower wings. On a copy, Georg pasted on the Gorgefield logo and covered it with White-Out until even the *G,* whose arc formed the curve of the earth and whose crossbar formed the fuselage of an airplane, could only dimly be made out. He had Fran make a copy of this copy, and to accompany it wrote a short letter on Fran's typewriter:

> *Dear Sirs: The enclosed document might interest you. The entire set will be offered for thirty million. Will you bid? Someone who understands the situation and has complete authority will be available for a meeting in San Francisco. Place and time of the meeting will be furnished to you next Wednesday at 10 a.m. Have your telephone operator expect a message with the code name "Rotors." The deal must be concluded by Friday of next week.*

He mulled over whether he should address the letter to "Dear Sir or Madam" or just "Dear Sirs," and whether the code name "Rotors" was good enough, but both issues were unimportant. Beneath the address, he simply wrote "Re: Attack Helicopter." He put the letter and the prepared copy in the envelope, addressed it to the Soviet embassy in Washington, and on Wednesday evening dropped it in a mailbox. He did this in the dead of night with Jill on his arm. He sat for a long time in front of a lamp with the negatives Fran had brought, trying to assess their authenticity and completeness. When he rolled them up again and stuck them in the cans, he wasn't much the wiser.

On Saturday he booked a flight to San Francisco for himself and Jill. He wanted to meet the Russians on Wednesday, but wanted to talk first with Buchanan, Benton's contact at Gorgefield Aircraft. But before that, he wanted to find a place where he could meet with the Russians. He would need two days to prepare.

After Fran gave up hope of changing Georg's mind, she tried to stay out of his way. He was prepared to respect that, but it was hard to do in the small apartment. They didn't utter a word as they sat opposite each other, or when they met at the door between the living room and the bedroom or in the hallway, letting the other go first or passing each other, barely touching, with Fran lowering her eyes: a withered intimacy that made Georg sad. But sometimes he was reminded of girls in ancient or distant cultures who have been promised to a man and are only allowed to show themselves to him after the wedding. Fran was again sleeping in the living room. Days ago, after their initial arguments, when she had aroused him but still had not been able to make him give up his plan, she made a point of sleeping in the living room.

On Friday evening he greeted her according to the ritual of the past week. In the morning he had gone shopping with Jill, also to accustom himself again to the outside world, and had spent the afternoon in the kitchen. He prepared a Cucuron dinner: tapenade on toast, duck Provençale, and chocolate mousse. She was withdrawn and taciturn, and avoided his glance. Later she didn't come to him in bed. But in the morning he found in his suitcase a baby sling with which he could strap Jill to his chest.

41

AT THE BEGINNING OF THE FLIGHT Jill screamed. She fell asleep when her screaming no longer attracted the other passengers' sympathy, but their exasperation. A little four-year-old girl tried to interest Jill in picture books and chocolates. An elderly woman gave Georg advice about bringing up children, especially young ladies. The stewardesses brought blankets, kept diapers handy, warmed bottles, and said "coochy-coo." They spoiled Jill, and they spoiled Georg.

In San Francisco they were picked up by Jonathan and Fern. A friend from Georg's student years in Heidelberg had studied at Stanford and shared an apartment in San Francisco with Jonathan, who was a painter, and when Georg had phoned his friend with his request, the friend had arranged for him to stay in Jonathan's apartment. Georg hadn't wanted to stay in a hotel with Jill. Besides, Jonathan's girlfriend Fern, an actress, was between jobs and was willing to look after Jill whenever Georg was taking care of his business. She took charge of Jill even before Georg wanted to let her go.

It had been raining in New York when they left, but in San Francisco the sun was shining in a clear blue sky. He left Jill in the renovated warehouse in which Fern and Jonathan were living with a cat and a Doberman, near the bay. The afternoon was before him, and he wanted to start looking for a place to rendezvous with the Russian.

It was clear what kind of place it should be. He wanted to be able to see whether the man was coming alone, so the place had to be open. Georg wanted to be sure that the man couldn't follow him, so he would have to be able to disappear into a crowd near the place, or be able to reach a parked car on a lightly traveled street. He would drive off, and, if he didn't see in the rearview mirror a car following him, he would take one of several detours and lose himself in the tangle of streets. That was how he imagined his getaway. Or, alternatively, that he would disappear into the crowd and get to a public toilet and disguise himself again. It would have to be sufficient to shake off one or more Russians. If the Americans had intercepted his letter and listened in on his phone call on Wednesday, and sent hundreds of men and helicopters after him, he wouldn't have a chance anyway.

He rented a car, got a map of the city, and drove off. At first he drove aimlessly, wherever the flow of traffic or the signs and one-way streets took him. He drove through long streets with two- and three-story apartment buildings. They were of brightly painted wood and adorned with bay windows, gables, and little towers. Business and neon signs suddenly jutted out between the first and second stories, advertising delis, Pepsi-Cola, antiques, dry cleaning, auto-repair shops, breakfast, self-service laundries, real estate, restaurants, picture framing, Budweiser, shoes, fashions, Coca-Cola, and more delis. The businesses and signs disappeared just as suddenly, followed by one apartment block after another. Georg drove through residential streets, shorter than those in Manhattan, the architecture more daring, the streets cleaner and emptier, and the small bits of nature greener. He drove over the hills of the city as excited as if he were on a roller-coaster ride. The topography didn't match the grid imposed on it, so they pointed up at the sky or down onto other streets. One moment he would be looking down at water, container ships, sailboats, and bridges, and another moment at the silhouettes of skyscrapers merging together at one end of the city, and the many arms with which freeways reached out over and between the buildings, over and under each other. He had the window open and the radio on, and let music and wind whistle about his ears. Sometimes he stopped, and stepped out like a tourist wanting to take a picture. But he only looked to see whether a small place was open enough, or a street lonely enough, or whether a staircase leading down from a steep, hilly street led only to a building or to the next street below.

On Sunday Georg forbade himself to look at the city map. He tried to get a feel for the city and its streets without it. He would have noted a suitable place on the map, but didn't find any. Still, by evening he had an idea of the peninsula, the ocean to the west, the bay to the east, the Golden Gate Bridge to the north. And he had an idea of how the city had originally grown up in the north, on the bay, and later proliferated over the rest of the peninsula.

On Monday morning, with the city map, he proceeded systematically. He drove through the parks and then along the coast of the Pacific. He found isolated places in Golden Gate Park, but their isolation could only shield them from surprise by a hiker, not a purposeful pursuer. The ocean beach stretched out long and open; gray clouds under a gray sky, gulls beating in the wind, a few joggers, a few hikers, a surfer who never got beyond the first wave, a yellow dredger piling up or carting off sand. But in front of the wall separating the road and the beach there were too many cars parked with people sitting in them. He went to an isolated hot-dog stand, and when the man fished the hot frankfurter from the pot of water the steam rose up in a dense cloud. It was cold here; in the morning Georg had started out from the building on the bay under a blue sky, and in the center of the peninsula had driven into the fog covering the Pacific Coast.

Then he thought he had found the place he was looking for. At the north end of the beach the land was hilly and the coast fell steeply to the sea, bending inward toward the Golden Gate Bridge and the bay. A street went up to the top of a hill, and Georg stopped in surprise in front of an acropolis. A square of low buildings and a classical arcade, and in the square in front a large circle with an empty fountain basin in the middle, and broad steps leading to the columned portico. He parked his car and walked around the circle. The sun had dissolved the clouds, and through the trees he looked down on the city, the ocean, and the twin red masts and arching roadway of the Golden Gate Bridge. Below him, two helicopters were flying along the shore. From the golf course, which came as far as the acropolis, one sometimes heard the strokes and voices of nearby players, or the soft hum of a golf cart. He could hear occasional cars in the distance coming closer and fading away again. Otherwise it was completely quiet. An enchanted place.

When he went up the steps to the portico he saw that this acropolis was an art museum, and that it was closed on Mondays and Tuesdays. He could imagine the cars that would be parked here side by side on Wednesday. And to destroy the enchanted mood, three cars drove up and disgorged a noisy Chinese or Japanese wedding party. He went back to his car. The bride was pretty.

On Monday evening he had grown tired of the city, but more tired of himself and his purposeful, meandering tourism. He liked the city's clarity that one could almost touch, its fresh cool breeze despite the relentless sunshine, the variety of its districts, cultures, and enticements. He thought one might portray San Francisco as a seductive virgin in starched frills, a virgin simultaneously flaunting and withholding her charms, while New York was an old hag, heavy and squat, sweating, steamy, stinking, babbling incessantly, sometimes screaming. But he was also sick of his perceptions and his useless sensibility. He hadn't found the place he was looking for. He parked the car and went to Jonathan and Fern's place. Jill was still awake; he gave her her bottle and changed her diaper on the long table in the kitchen, where he could roll her right and left. He tried to teach her to crawl. She crowed with pleasure. Then he put her down in the wide bed he shared with her. He was anxious lest she fall out, or that he would roll over on her. She followed him into his dreams.

Jonathan and Fern were cooking, and invited Georg to dinner. Cordial and interested, they asked what his business was. He suffered from his evasive answers, again longing to be normal and open. The couple was happy, although Fern was between jobs and Jonathan had had to interrupt his painting to earn some money. Then all three of them drank too much, and Jonathan became loud and boisterous, took his pistol out of a desk drawer, and shot out the streetlight across the street. Fern laughed and played along, but knew how to let Jonathan know when it was time to go to bed. Georg, too, longed for a relationship that would make him feel as whole and accepted as Fern's. What the hell, he thought, I long for Fran, whether or not she accepts me or pushes me away. I long to have the life with her that we only lived the shadow of in Cucuron and New York. And if living with Fran is like Fran herself, and there's nothing left to discover behind what I see and know, nothing more to awaken with a kiss, then I want and like what I see and know.

Everything else could go to hell, he thought: Joe, Mermoz, and Gorgefield, his revenge, the big money. He knew that the next day he would go on looking for the meeting place, drive to Gorgefield, and speak with Buchanan. He realized that the two things didn't go together or belong together, just like the clarity and intoxication in his head.

42

THE NEXT MORNING GEORG found himself alone in bed. Fern had left him a note that she was letting him sleep in and had taken Jill to go walking with the dog. In his pajamas he strolled through the apartment with a cup of coffee, looking at Jonathan's paintings.

They were big oil paintings, six by nine feet and larger, in dark, matte colors out of which shone through, here and there, the glowing blue or red of the pattern of a carpet. They showed a nude at the desk, a nude on the sofa, a nude sitting on the floor with her back leaning against the wall, an empty room in which the torso of a man sleeping on the floor stood out against the wall. All the paintings radiated coldness, as if the air in those rooms were thin and the people frozen in their attitudes. Georg took a gulp of hot coffee. Or had Jonathan painted the pictures with painfully restrained passion, the paintings turning lifeless in the process? The next painting was of the back of a television set and a couple: she was sitting on the sofa looking at the screen, while he was standing behind the sofa and turning to leave. Or does Jonathan want to prove that communication is impossible and loneliness unavoidable? Then there were paintings of nature, a glacier landscape in front of which two men were locked in combat; a meadow with a couple sitting, more next to each other than with each other; a forest clearing in which a man is kneeling, holding and kissing a little girl. Now Georg saw the paintings from a different angle. Jonathan didn't want to prove that loneliness was unavoidable, but everything went to show that it was, whether he wanted it to or not, presumably even against his will and against his attempts to capture and represent closeness. The closed eyes of the man kissing the little girl didn't express self-abandon but tension; the girl seemed to want to run away.

Georg remembered how Fran had given Jill her breast, and how he hadn't seen any closeness, warmth, or intimacy in it. Am I the man for whom loneliness has become unavoidable, communication impossible, even the perception of communication? A pack of cigarettes was lying on the table. He lit one. In New York one day he had simply stopped smoking. Now, after weeks of not smoking, the first deep draw was like a blow to his throat and his chest. He took another draw, went into the kitchen, held the cigarette under the running water, and threw it in the trash can.

The door to Jonathan's bedroom was open, and Georg went in. Outside the window, at the level of the sill, was a terrace covered with gravel. He climbed out and looked down at the tops of the trucks and shipping containers of the transport company, and across the way at a loading dock; behind it were warehouses, the insulators and wires of an electricity substation, a tall chimney. And he looked down a street that led to the bay and ended there in an earthen berm. Georg swung himself up onto the roof above Jonathan's bedroom and stood there. It was a corner building; Georg could see the intersection and had an unobstructed view of all four streets and, farther away, a view of a hill, a freeway, and a gas tank.

There it is! Georg thought, that's the place I'm looking for! The street leading to the bay must be Twenty-fourth Street, the cross street is Illinois, and its parallel street is Third. I have the Russian take a cab to the corner of Third and Twenty-fourth streets and walk east to the end of Twenty-fourth. From up here I can see the cab stopping on the corner, the Russian walking up Twenty-fourth, and also see if beforehand or at the same time a suspicious car appears and stops on Twenty-fourth Street or Illinois, where there's never much traffic.

Georg swung himself down. He got dressed and went out. When he stood on the earthen berm, he realized that it must be what was left of a park. Benches, paths, a dock for fishing, two blue port-o-johns, brown grass, and brown bushes. To the left was a short canal; behind it, old trolley cars, the warehouses again, and the chimney of a now audibly humming power plant. To the right was a fenced-in plot with construction material and machines, open ground with man-high underbrush, garbage, and automobile carcasses; farther off, green, yellow, red, and blue shipping containers, broad-legged container cranes, searchlights, and cables. In front of Georg was the bay, which stank of tar and dead fish, and in the distant haze the other shore.

Georg walked along the shore, fought his way through the underbrush, and in its shelter followed the fence that initially led along the shore and then back to Illinois Street. He had thought he'd find Twenty-fifth Street here, but instead came upon railroad tracks leading across a broad expanse to a derelict pier. A dog was wandering about. The wind stirred up dust.

The place was ideal. After the meeting, Georg could observe the Russian going back to Third Street, while he himself could return unobserved through the underbrush to Illinois Street where, covered by the parked cars, he could get back to the entrance of his building. But what if accomplices didn't turn up before the Russian or with him, but surrounded the place during the meeting?

Georg decided to have the Russian take a taxi to the corner of Third and Twenty-fourth streets, walk to the end of Twenty-fourth Street, and wait for a motorboat behind the earthen berm. He would recommend rubber boots. Then the accomplices would go back and forth on the bay with motorboats and binoculars.

Georg had originally thought to show the Russian the negatives in two meetings. He thought it better not to have all fourteen film cans with him at once. But now he had another idea. The place was good for one meeting but not for two, and he didn't have a place for a second meeting. He had to take care that the Russian didn't overpower him and take the negatives. He had noticed where Jonathan kept his pistol in the desk.

So, thought Georg, tomorrow: call around ten, arrange to meet at eleven. Give just enough time for the embassy in Washington to alert their man in San Francisco. But what if the people in Washington hadn't made any preparations, hadn't sent anyone to San Francisco, hadn't taken the letter seriously? *If, if, if.* Me and my ifs! A man was murdered on account of these negatives. They are valuable. Why shouldn't the Russians take the offer seriously?

43

GEORG DROVE TO PALO ALTO, where Gorgefield Aircraft had its offices and research laboratories. He hadn't made an appointment with Buchanan, since he didn't want a phone conversation that would give him only an incomplete picture of what he wanted to tell him, but enough for him to reach for the phone and call Benton.

Georg took U.S. Route 101 south. All eight lanes were filled with cars. Where are all these people going? And why don't I ever wonder that when I'm on a highway in France or Germany? Is it because the traffic flows differently here? People don't drive the same here; they're not only slower because of the speed limit, but also calmer. Hardly anyone passes anyone else. The cars glide smoothly next to one another, sometimes pulling ahead, sometimes falling back, like driftwood on a wide placid stream: as if it wasn't a matter of getting from one place to another as quickly as possible, as if life was about driving, not staying put.

At Palo Alto he exited the highway. Gorgefield Aircraft was on Alpine Road; after houses with green gardens, streets with green trees, and shops with blossoming flowers and shrubs by their entrances and around their display windows, the street led up into hills covered with grass of a burned golden brown. As the road coiled farther and farther up the hill there were no more houses, no trees, and hardly any cars. A large granite rock inlaid with a bronze company logo stood at the intersection where he turned off to Gorgefield. After another bend he looked down on a wide green valley. The road ended in a loop, on three sides of which stood five-story buildings made of granite or that had granite facades. On the fourth side a parking lot stretched out left and right by the entryway. Sprinklers were spinning on the green lawns; through the open car window he could hear them hissing, and saw rainbow-colored sunbeams in the spray.

He parked and went to the main entrance, where laurel trees stood in containers. The hall wasn't cool, it was freezing. He shivered. The doorman looked like a policeman: a badge on his shirtsleeve, a name tag on his breast pocket, a gun on his belt. He asked Georg for identification, but since Georg couldn't confirm that he had an appointment with Buchanan and wouldn't tell him the reason he wanted to see him, the guard didn't let him through. Finally the guard called Buchanan and handed Georg the receiver.

"Mr. Buchanan?"

"Yes. Who is this?"

"My name is Georg Polger. You don't know me, but what I have to tell you is quite important. I'd like a brief word with you, but not on the phone. Could you have me sent up? Or come down yourself if you prefer. As far as I'm concerned, the guard can frisk me for weapons, and feel free to bring some weapons yourself—I don't want to kill you, I just want to talk with you."

"Could you pass me over to the guard?"

Georg heard the guard say "Yes, sir" a number of times, after which another guard escorted him to Buchanan's office on the third floor. Buchanan's secretary served him a cup of coffee, had him wait for a while, and then took him in to Buchanan. He was a small, stocky, middle-aged man wearing a short-sleeved shirt with a tie. He had a strong handshake and numerous spider veins on his cheeks. He offered Georg the chair in front of his desk, and looked at him inquiringly.

"My story will sound incredible, but it's not important right now whether you believe it or not. The main thing is that you remember it so you can recall it when the time comes. Because when the time comes it will be too late to be telling it for the first time. Do you follow?"

It was only when Georg asked the question that he noticed that Buchanan was slightly cross-eyed. One of his eyes simply couldn't listen to Georg with interest.

"Go on," Buchanan said.

"I'm German, West German. As I'm sure you know, the partition of Germany has divided many families. Half my family lives in East Germany, among them my cousin. He works for the Stasi, what you might call the East German CIA. In fact, you could say he's not working for the Stasi right now, but for the Soviets. You know that the Soviets have the East Germans under their thumb, just as they do the Poles, the Czechs, the Hungarians, and the Bulgarians. That's also the case when it comes to these countries' secret services. Now to my point: my cousin has been given a mission that has taken him from France to the United States. The Russians are interested in the design of an attack helicopter that either the Europeans will build under the leadership of Mermoz, or you here in the United States. I don't know what measures the Russians have undertaken to get hold of the design plans, but my cousin informed me that an American has surfaced offering to sell the plans for thirty million dollars."

"Who?"

"I'll get to that in a moment. First, I'd like to show you what my cousin has given me. Does this mean anything to you?" Georg took a can of film out of his bag and put it on Buchanan's desk. "Feel free to open it and have a look."

Buchanan put on his glasses, opened the can, took out the negatives, held them up in front of the window, and slowly unfurled them. "Yes, this does mean something to me."

"I am to ask if you are prepared to pay for the pertinent background information. My cousin intends to defect to the West—next year, or the year after—and could do with a nest egg. He would inform you when he finds out who the American seller is and has proof. Perhaps he can even arrange a meeting and call you on short notice."

"All I can say is that this is a very strange story," Buchanan said, puckering his lips and rubbing his chin.

"I'm aware of that, as is my cousin. But there's no risk for you. At worst, it would be a waste of your time, at best you could—for a price we still have to discuss—locate and secure a hole in your system. By the way, here's something my cousin told me to give you." Georg took two photocopies out of his bag and placed them in front of Buchanan. They were identical, except for the lower right side where on one copy was Mermoz's double-decker logo, barely visible, and on the other, the Gorgefield airplane circling the world.

"And why, if I might ask, would I want two copies of the same thing?"

"I have no idea," Georg said, leaning back in his chair. "So what do you say?"

"You mean about the money?"

"Yes."

Buchanan shrugged his shoulders. "What sum does your cousin have in mind?"

"He says that the whole set is on sale for thirty million," Georg replied, taking the negatives from the desk, rolling them up, and putting them back in the can. "He doesn't want that much from you, since he says you've already paid. He's thinking one million."

"Just a lousy million, because we're supposed to have already paid a lousy thirty?" Buchanan again rubbed his chin. "That doesn't add up. Why would your cousin tell us what we need to know with nothing but a promise from me to you that he'll be paid? What court in the world could he turn to to get his million?"

"He'll turn to the press. If you don't pay, he'll sell his story to the papers. He thinks that isn't an option you'd be particularly pleased with."

"So that's what he thinks? Well, tell your cousin we'll pay the million." He looked at Georg warily. "Or should we first of all focus on you?"

"What more do you want to know?"

"I know you've told us everything that this cousin of yours has commissioned you to tell us, and that you don't know more. But perhaps you're not your cousin's cousin after all, but your cousin in person: the only cousin in this game. Or if your cousin does exist, perhaps you can give us a bit more background. I imagine you and he must be in contact. Might your cousin in fact be your uncle?" Buchanan looked at Georg sharply.

Georg laughed. "If I don't have a cousin, how could I be a cousin myself? But jokes aside, why would I want to play charades? As for my being in contact with him, the way it works is that *he* calls *me*."

Buchanan raised his hands and slapped them against the desk. "Damn! Do you know what happened to me this morning? I gave away the wrong puppy. My golden retriever had a litter, and six pups are more than I can handle. I wanted to keep one, but, believe it or not, by mistake I gave away the one I wanted to keep."

"So why don't you ask for it back?"

"Ask for it back? Ask for it back? I gave it to my boss. Am I supposed to tell him the puppy's too good for him? That he can have one of the others?"

Georg got up. "It's been a pleasure meeting you. Good luck with the puppy."

"You don't seem to give a damn about what happens to the puppy," Buchanan said, walking Georg to the door. "Good-bye."

Georg sped down the winding mountain road with his radio turned up all the way. His shirt fluttered in the wind. "It worked!" he yelled triumphantly. "This is the beginning of the end for you, Joe Benton! It doesn't matter what Buchanan thinks of my story, but, believe me, he'll be less and less pleased with your side of things!" Georg imagined Buchanan giving Benton the sack: "You're such an idiot, Benton! You were underhanded in your dealings—it doesn't matter in how many ways, but you were underhanded. I have no time for people like you!" Georg thought, the one thing that upsets me is that you'll probably never find out that I was the one who dug your grave! Buchanan won't tell you about me, just as you didn't tell him about me either. But who cares! Georg chuckled. And now for the Russians. And why not bring in the Chinese too, the Libyans, the Israelis, the South Africans? It's like a cocktail where you throw in all kinds of spicy things: one sip and you hit the roof. If the world wants to dance to a crazy tune, it might as well be mine!

Jill brought Georg back down to earth. She was lying on the bed with her eyes wide open. She had vomited and was whimpering. Fern's diagnosis was an upset stomach. Georg could only see that the poor baby was suffering, and he had a bad conscience. Fern suggested he give her some Coca-Cola.

"What do you mean?" he asked.

"If you have an upset stomach, you drink Coca-Cola. Everyone does it. My mother even had a little bottle of Coca-Cola syrup always handy."

"You're not seriously suggesting I give Jill Coca-Cola! How old were you when your mother used that household remedy on you?" *Household remedy!* Georg had to force himself even to use the words. Household remedies were wormwood, chamomile and linden blossom tea, compresses, and alcohol rubs. Coca-Cola as a household remedy! America really was a new world.

Fern was exasperated. "You can't expect me to remember if I was given Coca-Cola when I was two months old, but I was given it ever since I can remember."

They got a can out of the refrigerator. Georg picked Jill up, dipped his finger in the brown liquid, and then popped it in her mouth. She sucked at his finger, and he repeated it a second time and then a third.

"Do you think that's enough?" he asked.

Fern had been watching carefully. She flicked a lock of hair out of her face and said with conviction, "Five should do the trick."

He dipped his finger two more times, and then carried Jill onto the terrace, through the rooms, down the stairs to the laundry room, and back up the stairs. He kept mumbling softly to her, telling her fairy tales and crooning lullabies. By the time he got back to the terrace, she was asleep. He sat down carefully on the edge of the deck chair and looked down the street, counting five abandoned car wrecks and three sailboats in the bay. He watched a dirigible heading north.

44

ON WEDNESDAY, AT PRECISELY TEN in the morning, Georg called the Soviet embassy in Washington from a pay phone.

"Embassy of the USSR, can I help you?"

"I would like to leave a message under the code name 'Rotors.' Have your man in San Francisco take a cab to the corner of Twenty-fourth and Third streets, then walk east on Twenty-fourth all the way to the end. Have him wait there for a motorboat that will appear at eleven. Did you get all that?"

"Yes, but . . ."

Georg hung up. It took him ten minutes to get back home. He didn't hurry; it would take a good fifteen minutes for the embassy in Washington to contact its man in San Francisco and tell him where to go. Fern and Jill were at the Golden Gate Park, and Jonathan barely looked up from a new painting he was working on as Georg went over to the desk. "If you want some paper, it's in the top left-hand drawer," Jonathan said. Georg took the gun out of the bottom right-hand drawer. It was still unclear what Jonathan's new picture was to be of.

By twenty past ten Georg was lying on the roof. Illinois and Twenty-fourth streets were quiet. From time to time he saw a van, trucks with or without containers, construction machinery, and delivery vehicles. For ten whole minutes there was no car, then at ten-thirty a police car drove slowly up Illinois Street, made a U-turn at the intersection, and slowly drove back down. At ten-thirty-five a big, squat Lincoln turned onto Twenty-fourth Street from Third. Its exhaust pipe rattled and its springs groaned as it drove over the rough pavement of the intersection. The Lincoln came to a halt at the end of Twenty-fourth Street. Nobody got out. Dense traffic was rumbling on Third Street and on the highway beyond.

Georg was nervous. The police car. The Lincoln. What he needed was two pairs of eyes so he could watch both the intersection in front of him and the Lincoln behind him. He kept asking himself whether the Russians were playing along, or whether they thought all this was just a prank—or a trap. "Wait and keep cool," he said to himself. "What kind of a prank could this be, or what kind of trap? The Americans could hardly corner a Soviet agent waiting by the bay for an unknown man."

To his relief, Georg saw the Lincoln backing up onto Twenty-fourth Street and then turn at the intersection and drive away along Third. It was quarter to eleven.

At ten to eleven a cab stopped at the corner of Third and Twenty-fourth. A man got out, paid through the open window, and looked around. Having gotten his bearings, he walked toward the intersection. With every step Georg could see him more clearly. He wasn't one of those Soviet musclemen with white blond hair and Slavic cheekbones, but a thin, balding, older man in a dark blue suit with a blue-and-white striped shirt and a patterned tie. He walked carefully, as if he had recently sprained his ankle.

There were no backup men following him, stealthily hiding behind parked cars. Georg could hear the man's footsteps as he walked past the terrace, one foot with a strong tread, the other with a light shuffle. He saw him go to the end of Twenty-fourth Street and disappear behind the berm. Again Georg's eyes scanned the streets, the parked cars, the wrecks, but he didn't see anything suspicious. It was five to eleven.

He climbed down from the roof onto the terrace, grabbed his jacket, in which the pistol lay heavily in a side pocket, and hurried down the stairs. He opened the front door a crack and peered out at the intersection one more time. There was no sign of the distinguished-looking gentleman.

Georg walked down Twenty-fourth Street and up the berm. The man was standing on the shore looking out on to the bay. Georg put his foot up on the berm, rested his elbow on his knee, and waited. After a while the man turned and looked back, saw Georg, and came up to him. As they stood facing each other Georg noticed that his tie was covered with a host of tiny white garden gnomes—standing, sitting, lying—all wearing pointed red hats.

"Shall we stay here?" the Russian said, eyeing Georg over the rimless spectacles perched on his nose. He looks like a professor, Georg thought.

"Yes, here's fine," Georg replied. He took his hand with the pistol out of his pocket. "May I?" He frisked the "professor," who stood there shaking his head. Georg found no weapon.

"Doesn't one do this sort of thing?" Georg asked with a smile. "I'm not up on the etiquette of this kind of meeting." They sat down. "I've brought along the merchandise," Georg continued, taking out the can with the negatives and giving them to the professor. "There are, altogether, fourteen rolls of film."

The professor took the negatives out of the can and held them up to the sky. He slowly eyed one frame after another. Georg looked at the sailboats. When the professor was finished with the first roll, he handed it back without comment and Georg gave him the next. Two boats, one with red sails and one with blue, were racing past. A ship with an array of brightly colored containers on its deck came by, then a fast, gray warship. Georg kept handing him can after can. The sun glittered on the shivering waves.

"What price are you asking?" the professor inquired in a thin, high voice, pronouncing the words with a clipped British intonation.

"My party prices them at thirty million, and anything over twenty is mine. If it's under twenty, I'll have to check back with my party."

The professor carefully rolled the last roll of film tighter and tighter, until it would have fit into the can five times. He slid it into the can and held it there with his finger. "Tell your party that we have been offered the same negatives for twelve million, and that we find even that price too high." He let go of the roll, and it expanded to the confines of the can with a hiss.

Georg was struck dumb. What the professor had just said was unthinkable. What did it mean? What if it was true? What if it wasn't? "I will inform my party. But I don't see them believing that there is another offer—they will see that as a ploy on your part to lower the price."

The professor smiled. "The matter is more complicated than you seem to realize. Were you to view the matter from our perspective, with the premise that the first seller does in fact exist, you will see that just as you have doubts about the existence of the first offer, we have reason to doubt the existence of a bona fide second offer that you are presenting. Not to put too fine a point on it, the crux of the matter not only hinges on the contingence you have surmised—that a potential buyer who has two offers might pitch them against each other—but a seller for his part can also influence the negotiations to his advantage by stepping up to the negotiating table, so to speak, and donning the garb of yet another seller."

How could anyone formulate such sentences! The logic behind what the professor was saying was as immaculate as his grammar.

"Why don't you simply decide what the designs are worth to you and name a price?" Georg said.

Now the professor laughed. "You must admit there is something ironic in the idea that someone like me should be called upon to explain the capitalist law of supply and demand and the connection between demand, price, and value. But let us shed light on another aspect of this matter. Let us suppose that you are requesting for your private use any moneys that exceed a sum that, as you inform us, your party sets at twenty million, but which, circumstances being what they are, should realistically be set at fifteen. And if we also take as a premise that you will not be able to count on our closing a deal with a sum beyond twenty-one million, as you yourself have, in a sense, intimated, then I put it to you that you are facing a personal profit in the range of one to six million dollars—a sum, I might add, that doubtless is far more manageable. Do you follow me?"

"It was hard to follow, but I find it's worth the effort. I see you like balancing 'ifs' with 'thens.' Is that just in speaking, or in action as well?"

"Do you know the story of Alexander the Great and the Gordian knot?" the professor said.

"Why do you ask?"

"Well, in the Gordian fortress one day, Alexander the Great happened upon a great knot that no one had ever managed to unravel. The upshot was that Alexander simply took his sword and cut through the knot. Logic, you see, is a matter of unraveling chains of thought and meaning that in our everyday communication become tangled, and as the links in these chains are the 'ifs' and 'thens,' then this very game of 'ifs' and 'thens'—as you have it—serves to unravel as opposed to cutting through such tangles.

By extension, it also has as its focal point talking and thinking as opposed to acting. If you will allow me to point the moral of that story and regard it through the prism of you, me, our interested parties, and the merchandise in question, then our aforementioned deliberations place you in the role of Alexander the Great who is faced with the knot and the alternative of attempting, like so many prior visitors to the Gordian palace, to unravel it or simply cut through it with the swipe of his sword."

"Those are your aforementioned deliberations, not mine."

The professor had lifted the can, holding it between his index and middle fingers, and with his last words had dropped it into Georg's open palm. The professor shrugged his shoulders. "My deliberations, our deliberations—by now, I would say, these deliberations have taken root in your mind too, and are consequently as much *your* deliberations as *ours*."

"Do you know the other seller?" Georg asked.

"Do I know him?"

"Have you seen him, or spoken to him? Do you know who he is?"

The professor shook his head. "He didn't leave a calling card, nor did he show us his passport."

"Any hunches who he might be?"

"Ah, the breaking through the borders of knowledge by hunches—indeed, one could describe our trade in those very terms. We most definitely have hunches, and our hunches, like all hunches, would be worthless if we had nothing to base them on. If the issue at hand is that you are uncertain about the loyalty within your faction, then I would like to assure you that I understand your position. But as I am not responsible for garnering the hunches particular to this case, I can only say that I will make inquiries and inform myself of the current state of hunches."

"I didn't say that I have any issues of loyalty with my party."

"Indeed you didn't," the professor replied.

"I might have asked you this question purely in order to clarify my party's interests."

"Indeed."

"So, under no circumstances would you pay twelve million, but would definitely pay six. Am I right?" Georg asked.

The professor took his time answering. "Your party, to whom you must decide how much or how little of this conversation you will report, is urging us to close by Friday. That's the day after tomorrow. The other seller is not as impatient. I don't wish to intimate that a quick closure is out of the question—in fact, it might very well be the most apt solution. But as we have already touched on the issue of competition, we should also touch on the time factor. Let me put this in refreshingly direct American terms: the sooner you want to see cash, the less cash you'll see."

"Will you be in town until Friday?" Georg asked.

"I most certainly will."

"Where can I reach you?"

"Call the Westin St. Francis, and ask for room 612."

"You'll hear from me," Georg said.

The professor nodded and left. Georg watched him until he disappeared around the corner of Third Street. Then Georg made his way through the underbrush, reached the cover of the parked cars, and got to Fern and Jonathan's front door. It was a quarter to twelve.

The other offer that the professor had mentioned kept going through Georg's mind; was Georg trying to get Joe entangled in an affair in which he had long been involved? If the other offer was real, then all the facts pointed to Joe. Furthermore, the professor's proposal that Georg close the deal with a few million and bail out was working irresistibly on his mind. Should I quit trying to expose Joe? The money issue had always been at the back of

Georg's mind. His dream had been that at the end of all this Joe would be finished and he would be rich: all's well that ends well. How he could get his hands on the money was unclear, though how he could finish Joe off was very clear indeed, and Georg had set his priorities accordingly. But now suddenly both goals seemed within reach. Or is it, he said to himself, that I want it all, as Fran pointed out the other day, and hence want too much?

He drove to Golden Gate Park and looked for Jill and Fern. He couldn't find them. He drove to the shore and went for a run along the beach. He ran with wonderful lightness, until his legs practically gave way and he fell onto the sand. He lay there until he felt a chill. By evening he knew that he wouldn't risk the money just to settle accounts with Joe.

45

GEORG WOKE UP AT FIVE in the morning. The house was rumbling and shaking. He went to the window. A long freight train was rolling by. The engine's eyes threw white light onto the tracks, which Georg had seen from the street but not paid attention to. A pulsating red signal lit up the abandoned cars and trucks along the roadside. The train rattled past beneath his window, black and heavy. A worker stood on the platform of the last car, swinging a lamp. Georg leaned out and saw the lights of the train grow smaller and fainter, and heard the deep, dull warning signal the locomotive emitted at every crossing grow softer.

Jill was asleep. He lay down next to her and watched the brightening dawn. The phone in the kitchen began ringing and wouldn't stop. As Jill grew restless, he got up and answered.

"Hello?"

"Is that you, Georg?"

"Fran! How the hell did you . . ."

"Your friend in Germany told me where you were. You had jotted down his number on a pad and I called him. He told me where you are. Listen, Georg, you've got to get out of there. Joe wants to . . . Joe realized that the negatives were missing. He looked in the safe and they weren't there, so he knew that I had . . . What could I do but tell him what I did? I had to tell him everything. He says he's going to get Jill and bring her back. Are you there, Georg? He's on his way to the airport. He swore he wouldn't do anything to you, but he was so mad and looked so crazy. Georg, you've got to get out of there! Leave Jill where she is, please don't take her with you. But you have to get out! All night I've been wondering if I should call you, or if you'd use my call against me. You must leave Jill and me alone. I can't handle this anymore. I don't want anything to happen to you, but I want Jill back. I'm really scared."

"Don't worry, Fran, I won't take her with me. Don't be scared. She's doing fine here, there's a dog and a cat she likes, and everyone's being really sweet to her. How does Benton intend to get her?"

"He says there's no way you can have her with you all the time, so you can't really use her as a hostage. He'll get at her when you're out somewhere without her. He's taking one of his men along."

"Do you know when he's arriving?"

"He's leaving now, on the Pan Am flight from JFK. He'll be in San Francisco by noon. Will you promise you'll be gone by the time he gets there, and that there'll be no trouble when he comes to take Jill away?"

"Don't be afraid, Brown Eyes. There's no need to be afraid. Jill won't be in any danger, and I won't cause problems. You'll have her back, and when she's grown up you can tell her the story of the crazy guy who ran off with her, and she can tell all her friends that when she was a baby she had been abducted by someone who had run off with her to San Francisco. Hey, Brown Eyes, don't cry."

She hung up. Georg turned on the coffeemaker and took a look at Jonathan's new painting. The day before there had only been the tree trunks of a dark forest with the rough outline of a man, crouching or kneeling, his arm gently hugging the shoulder of a girl. Jonathan must have worked late into the night. The man's head was finished. His mouth was whispering something into the girl's ear, his brown eyes exuding warmth and humor, as if they wanted to share with the viewer the anticipation at how happy the little girl would be at his whispered words. Her face was beaming, her shoulders raised shyly. The girl was still an outline, but the man's head brought her alive.

This one's a winner, Jonathan! The air in your painting is no longer thin, the people no longer wooden. Perhaps happy paintings don't sell as well as paintings of horror, because everyone who is happy is the same, or, as Tolstoy puts it: only in suffering is one an individual and interesting, or perhaps one merely feels that way, or, whatever, I can't remember his exact words. Either way, I'm standing in front of your new painting and know that I'm not sentenced to loneliness and being shut out from communicating with other people.

The coffeemaker had stopped hissing, and Georg went to the kitchen. He poured himself a cup of coffee and sat down at the end of the long table. Seven people could sit on each side, he counted; one could throw a dinner for sixteen. He looked out the window. The sky was blue. On the street the truck engines from next door were rumbling. Why did they all sound so different? Why doesn't one truck engine rumble like another? At night, when all the trucks are lined up, they look the same.

Don't try dodging the issues, weigh the situation! Why is Benton coming here? What does he think I'm doing with the negatives in San Francisco? Does he suspect that I got in touch with Gorgefield Aircraft? He's not coming here to talk. He could do that on the phone, or at least try. I doubt he's coming to talk to Gorgefield, either. He could do that on the phone too. Perhaps he did talk to him and didn't like what he heard. Is he coming here because of Jill? That's a stupid question. Even if Jill or Fran were important to him, he knows I wouldn't do anything to the baby. I doubt that even Fran sees me as a tiger, but Benton sized me up as a paper tiger right from the start.

No, that's not true. Though Benton knows I don't have it in me to be violent, I did corner him, identify him as a Polish or Russian secret agent, and, when that turned out not to be the case, I changed course and am now about to corner him again. He knows that—even if he doesn't know exactly what I'm doing and planning. He's scared. Particularly if *he* is planning to do business with the Russians.

What would I do in his position?

Georg got up slowly, went back into the big room that he thought of as Jonathan's studio, and looked for the cigarettes. He lit one and sucked in the smoke. He waited for it to rasp down his throat and chest, and it did. He sucked in another mouthful of smoke. He stood unseeing before Jonathan's paintings.

Benton wants to kill me.

He has nothing to lose and everything to gain. He might not have been pleased with the article in the *Times,* but if you think about it, both the article and the statements of those two officers, and the fact that I've abducted Jill, will help him create a scenario in which killing me could appear as a heroic act—or at least as necessary. And whatever damage I've done to Benton with Gorgefield Aircraft, any damage control on his part would be easier if I were dead. He doesn't want me alive and talking.

What am I going to do about this?

Run? Will I manage to get out of the United States? And wouldn't Benton track me down, even in Cucuron or Karlsruhe?

Georg studied the cigarette, which he was holding between the thumb, index, and middle fingers of his left hand. The smoke slid down the cigarette and rose in quick arabesques. Pall Mall. *In hoc signo vinces.* Two lions bearing a coat of arms. Georg laughed.

What about Fran? Fran, whom I love—don't ask me why. Fran, whom I want to be with even if it'll mean loneliness. Fran, whom I've begun to love even more through Jill, as if I weren't enough in love already. What will become of Fran and me if I run away?

Georg went to Jonathan's desk, took out the pistol, and weighed it in his hand. Cut through the Gordian knot? I don't even know how to load this thing or shoot it. You pull the trigger. Do I hold my shooting hand with the other one? Do I aim with the sights or rely on instinct? And isn't there such a thing as a safety catch?

Jonathan's bedroom door opened.

"Hi, Georg," Fern said, walking sleepily to the bathroom. Luckily she hadn't seen the pistol.

The day was beginning. The toilet flushed, and Fern came out of the bathroom. She got some coffee for herself and Jonathan. Jonathan showered. Georg showered. Jill screamed. Fern mixed some powdered milk, warmed it up, and gave it to Jill. Jonathan fried eggs and bacon, and they had breakfast. Georg felt as if he were experiencing these everyday joys for the last time: The bitter coffee, the hot stream of water on his body in the shower, the taste of the eggs and bacon, the coziness with which one talked about little everyday necessities. After breakfast, Georg for the first time put on the baby sling that Fran had packed for him, put Jill in it, and went for a walk.

Benton wants to kill me, he thought again.

Georg walked up the hill and showed Jill the buildings of the city, the highways, the bridges, and the bay. She fell asleep.

How can I tell Fern and Jonathan that this afternoon two men will come by to collect Jill? "By the way, Fern, there'll be these two guys knocking on your door, they'll be looking for Jill. They might even kick your door in, or threaten you and Jonathan, or pretend they are policemen: but just give them Jill, and don't worry about it. And thanks for looking after us, here's some money, bye."

Georg made his way back. What he did next he could not explain then or later, nor could he point to the thought or feeling that made him take that course of action. There was no sudden *click* in his mind. As he walked, he had been weighing how best to prepare Jonathan and Fern for Joe's visit, what he should leave behind for Jill and Joe, where he should drop his rental car, how he would get to the Greyhound bus station. He had even begun to fantasize about his journey to nowhere. But back at the house, he did none of those things. His hands and legs didn't do it, nor did his head—not that they refused to go along; refusal presupposes some form of resistance, and here there was no resistance. Georg simply went another way, things simply went another way.

As all smokers know, you can have stopped smoking for two years, left all symptoms of withdrawal behind, only rarely think of a cigarette, enjoy your existence and identity as a nonsmoker; but one day the nonsmoker smoker is sitting at his desk or on a park bench or in an airport lounge, and with no obvious reason, without being particularly stressed or particularly relaxed, gets up, walks over to a cigarette machine, buys a pack, and begins smoking again. Just like that. Relationships can begin or end this way too. It is the same principle with which one carefully studies a menu and decides on a filet of sole but orders tournedos.

Georg called Pan Am and asked when the first plane from New York was due to land. At ten o'clock. That gave him just two hours. He called the Gorgefield office and asked for Buchanan.

"Mr. Buchanan? My cousin came to see you the day before yesterday. I take it you know what this is in reference to?" Georg said, trying hard to imitate an East German accent, which, though it didn't sound authentic, was strange enough to pass.

"Well I'll be damned. . . ."

"I have a meeting set up at the San Francisco airport this morning," Georg said. "The seller is arriving at ten o'clock on the Pan

Am flight from New York. Bring the police with you, as I'm being followed and will need protection." Georg hung up, and then called the Westin St. Francis Hotel and asked for room 612. The phone rang a long time, and while he waited he divided 612 into 2 times 2 times 3 times 3 times 17.

"Hello?"

"Good morning," Georg said. "Did I wake you?"

"If I were still asleep at such an hour, it would be fitting for me to be woken up."

"Did you manage to find out more about the other seller?"

"I still haven't managed . . ."

"But I have. And you can have the negatives for two million. I don't know how much money you brought with you and in what denominations, but I would like you to place two million in small bills in a briefcase and to be at the airport at ten o'clock, at the Central Terminal, Departures. I'll give you the films and leave."

46

THE CENTRAL TERMINAL LIES above a two-story oval of roads into which the highways feed at the other end. The lower level is for arrivals, the upper for departures. On the lower level, only the front lobby is open to the public at large; beyond automatic sliding doors is a restricted customs area for arrivals. On the upper level, one can go all the way to where the wide terminal corridor begins, where the airplane gates are located. One can look through a glass wall down into the customs area.

Georg had set out immediately after making the phone calls. He found a parking spot near the entrance, and walked up and down the Central Terminal until he knew it well. From upstairs, I can see Joe first. But because he's coming from New York, he won't have to go through customs, and will pass through the hall quite quickly. He'll come through the arrivals door, won't stop at the cordoned-off area where people are waiting for passengers, but will turn either to the right, where the conveyor belts bring out the luggage, or head for the taxi stand or one of the car-rental desks. If the flight is on time, he'll be out by five past ten at the earliest, or a quarter past at the latest. So from the upper level I'll be able to see him first. The professor will be upstairs too, since I told him I was leaving. Buchanan will be waiting downstairs by the arrivals. I won't need more than a minute to go up and down between the two levels. From the upper level, where there's a view of the arrivals hall, there's no view of the area outside the sliding door, nor can anyone see the upper level from there.

Georg stood by the red ropes outside the arrivals area and looked up. Through a small atrium he could see the bays of a glass dome. The upper level rests on thick columns. A dome, columns—Georg smiled and thought, I see I can't get away from cathedrals. His smile was one of resignation. The professor would enjoy the "ifs" and "thens" of what I've set up here. If Joe wants to kill me, it's because I could be dangerous for him with Gorgefield Aircraft and perhaps even with the Russians. But if he sees that the cat is out of the bag, he'll have his hands full trying to deal with both the cat and the bag, and won't have time to focus on me. Then I'll come out of all this unscathed. Joe will be angry, but he won't kill me because he's angry.

That was Georg's plan: he would show himself with the professor upstairs so that Joe would see both of them when he came through the arrivals hall. Then Georg and the professor would proceed to the escalator leading to the lower level. And when Joe came out of the arrivals hall and saw Buchanan, Georg would throw from the escalator the fourteen film cans at their feet. He would let the professor continue down the stairs, while he would sprint back up the escalator and disappear. Joe, the professor, Buchanan, and the police could then deal with one another as they pleased.

Buchanan arrived at ten to ten. He arrived with two men who had the powerful build and expressionless faces typical of policemen and gangsters. Georg saw them from the top of the escalator. Buchanan said something to the two men and they disappeared behind the columns, while he went to stand by the red rope with all the people waiting for arriving passengers. From time to time he looked about discreetly.

The professor arrived at five to ten. He had the same careful tread, the same blue suit and striped shirt, but no tie. He was holding a briefcase in his hand.

"Are you taking the ten-twenty Pan Am flight to London?" he asked.

Georg shrugged his shoulders. "Come with me, I want to show you something," he said, nodding his head toward the glass wall above the customs area.

"Where are the goods?"

As he walked, Georg put his hands in his jacket pockets and pulled out some of the cans. He was walking fast. The monitor showed that the Pan Am flight had arrived.

Joe had the redhead with him. That's not surprising, Georg thought; after all, he knows me quite well. The redhead was carrying two bags. Joe was talking and gesticulating—a corpulent mass of affability.

"Do you know him?" Georg asked, nudging the professor and pointing at Joe. He didn't wait for an answer. He beat his fists against the glass wall. That action in itself might not have caught Joe's attention and made him look up, but the glass was secured, and a grating alarm went off. All heads in the area below looked up. Georg saw the surprise in Joe's face.

"What are you doing?" the professor asked, grabbing Georg's arm.

"Come on!" Georg shouted and, seizing the professor by the hand, began running, pushing, dodging people, and jumping over luggage, dragging the professor behind him. They reached the escalator and began to descend. He let go of the professor, who was gasping and cursing, and reached for the cans of film in his pockets. Buchanan came into sight, as did the door to the hall.

Georg's actions had not aroused any suspicions. A man bangs his hand against the glass wall, setting off a false alarm, and then runs with another man to the escalator. The two men running could be father and son, late and frantically making their way through the crowd. Nothing unusual in that.

It all happened in a flash. The glass door slid open, Joe came out of the arrivals area, Georg threw the cans. His aim was good: a few of them hit Joe, the others landed close by him. Joe looked at the cans, and then in the direction from which they had been flung.

The bullet hit Joe in the forehead. Georg saw him fall, saw Buchanan turn and aim again. So it's with both hands, Georg thought, you shoot with both hands. He saw Buchanan's face, his eyes, his tight lips, the gun's muzzle. He wanted to duck, but the shot rang out.

People screamed and ran for cover. Buchanan shouted something, Georg couldn't hear what. The professor, who had been standing above him on the escalator, fell onto him and slid down, collapsing onto a woman who was cowering next to Georg. Georg heard the rasping horror of her shrieks close to his ear.

Then he saw the briefcase, which had slipped out of the professor's hand. The escalator came to a halt. Georg automatically reached for the briefcase and scurried doggedly, hunched forward, up the escalator. He stepped on hands, pushed people out of the way, and at the top of the escalator elbowed his way through the crowd that had gathered to see what was going on downstairs. All these people had been near the atrium and heard the shots and screams. Those who were farther back hadn't noticed anything, and Georg casually walked past them and out of the building.

He drove back to San Francisco. He parked at the end of

Twenty-fourth Street, took the briefcase out of the car, and slowly walked to a bench near the waterfront. He sat down and put the briefcase at his feet. It was low tide, and rocks, car tires, and a refrigerator were looming out of the water.

He sat there for a long time, watching the sun's rays dancing on the waves. His mind was empty. Of course, he finally looked into the briefcase. And later, as Jill was asleep next to him, he turned on a table lamp and opened the briefcase again. It didn't contain two million. It didn't even contain one. He counted $382,460. There was a disarray of hundred-dollar bills mixed in with fifties and twenties, and between them the tie with the garden gnomes, tied and ready to be slipped on.

The following day all the newspapers featured the shooting at the airport. Georg read that Townsend Enterprises had been involved in industrial espionage for the Russians at Gorgefield Aircraft, and that Benton and a Russian agent had fallen into a trap set by Gorgefield Aircraft. Benton had attempted to shoot his way out, and had been shot dead by Buchanan. The Russian agent had been hospitalized, critically wounded. There was a picture of Richard D. Buchanan Jr., security adviser at Gorgefield, looking grim.

Georg read the newspaper the following morning at the airport. He was wearing sunglasses, and Jill was in the carrier sling. Nobody was paying particular attention. It was shortly before ten. The Pan Am flight from New York was scheduled to land soon. Fran had said that she would pick up Jill and take the one-thirty flight back to New York.

"Come and stay forever," Georg had told her.

She had laughed, but then had asked him what the weather was like. "Does it get cool there in the evenings?"

Epilogue

THEY DROVE SOUTH AND TOOK A FLIGHT from Mexico to Madrid, and from Madrid to Lisbon. Today they live in a house by the sea. Jill is five, and Fran sometimes tells her a bedtime story about a crazy guy who once upon a time ran off to San Francisco with her when she was a baby. They have two more children. Georg is translating again, because he couldn't go on doing nothing.

"Why didn't you write your story yourself?" I asked Georg, as we were sitting beneath the stars on his terrace above the sea. He had read my manuscript and was quibbling over this or that detail.

"Fran didn't want me to. This might sound strange, but since San Francisco we never talk about any of this. Fran won't have it." Georg laughed. "Whenever I bring up the subject she dismisses it as water under the bridge, and says she doesn't want me to spend weeks on end at my desk mulling over the past."

Georg poured more wine, Alvarinho from Monção, light on the palate but it goes straight to your head. He leaned back. By now he was almost entirely bald; the wrinkles on his forehead and around his mouth had turned into deep furrows, and the groove in his chin had become more pronounced. But he had a healthy complexion, and seemed relaxed and content.

"You know," he said, "I've come to realize that Fran is right. When I read your manuscript, everything was so distant, a faraway echo; you don't know whether it was your voice or someone else's. It's like when someone finds an old photograph of his father, who died young, and knows perfectly well that it's his father, even though he barely remembers him. When I told you about my final weeks in New York and San Francisco and you came up with the idea of turning it into a book, I was pleased. I thought that if I read what you had written I'd see things more clearly, that I'd see a structure and a pattern where I could . . . oh, I don't know. I was a real mess back then. But I guess it's true that we can never see clearly what we are doing or what happens to us, we can't even hold on to it. Sooner or later it ends up as water under the bridge—so I guess the sooner that happens, the better."

The summer after Georg's return from America, I was sitting at my desk in my apartment in the Amselgasse one evening when the downstairs bell rang. I wasn't expecting anybody, but buzzed whoever it was in. In our age of telephones, unexpected guests are rare. I looked down the stairwell, but recognized neither the hand that was groping its way up the banister nor the sound of his tread. When he came into sight on the landing below, I was quite relieved: after my visit to Cucuron in September I hadn't heard from Georg, except for a brief phone call from New York asking me urgently to send him some money. Not to mention that Jürgen had opened the sealed envelope Georg had sent him and had read to me Georg's predicament in New York, and I was afraid for his safety. His parents had no information about his whereabouts, he hadn't contacted the Epps again, nor had he been in touch with Larry or Helen, whose addresses the Epps had given me.

Georg and I hugged. I went to get some wine, and he told me all about New York and San Francisco, and about Fran, who was waiting for him in Lisbon. He talked all night. The sun came up, and I prepared a bed for him. He was in the shower, and I stood by the window smoking a final cigarette. Was I just tired? I couldn't believe his luck. Or was I jealous? He was doing great, he said, and Fran was perfect, Jill a treasure, and the money a blessing. He had fidgeted all night with his sunglasses, turning them about in his hands, putting them on, sliding them down to the edge of his nose, taking them off again, chewing on them, folding and unfolding them.

He had only come to Heidelberg for a short time. He was going to see his parents the following day and fly back to Portugal the day after. He had to be careful: not enough water had flowed beneath the bridge; they might still be after him. It was at breakfast that I told him I wanted to turn his story into a book. He liked the idea. But I should take my time, he said, it would be best for the book not to appear too soon; not to mention that names and places had to be changed. He again put on his sunglasses.

Some years passed. He called me from time to time, and once we met at the airport in Frankfurt. For a long time the notes I had made for the book lay tucked away in my drawer. I completed the manuscript a year ago, but couldn't send it to him, since he had never given me his address; then I recently got a call from him inviting me to Lisbon.

Fran picked me up at the airport. I didn't recognize her, but she recognized me. I had only met her once, briefly—in Cucuron, at Georg's party—and I'm bad at matching faces to photographs. I'd pictured her quite differently. Maybe it was also that she's changed, become somewhat matronly. He too strikes me as heavier and more settled.

While I was writing the book there were times when I asked myself whether this was a story of *amour fou*. But I saw the two of them together—with their children, in their house, their garden, cooking, eating, doing the washing up—I realized they were just living the quiet life that Françoise had always wanted to live. *Amour fou*, perhaps, but a quiet *amour fou*.

Georg was fiddling with his sunglasses again. He had worn them all day until dark. "There is something I noticed in the manuscript," he said, "that passed me by when it actually happened. Something I didn't understand at the time. You describe the exchange I had with Buchanan where he asks me if I am my cousin, and then asks if my cousin isn't in fact my uncle. He asked me that quite specifically, it all came back to me. When I read it, I was surprised that I'd told you about it and that you'd remembered it. It seemed like one of those weird, funny little details. But maybe it's neither funny nor weird. I'd always thought that Buchanan shot Joe and the professor because his foremost concern was the security of Gorgefield Aircraft, or because he didn't want a court case that would end up in a scandal for Gorgefield, or that he hated Benton for double-crossing him, or simply because he was trigger-happy. I thought it would be one or all of the above—or something along those lines—and that he meant to shoot me, not the professor."

"He saw you and thought this proved you were the Russian agent, that the cousin story was just a cover, and that in fact there was no cousin—which there wasn't."

"But there *was* an uncle," Georg insisted, "the uncle Buchanan asked me about, the uncle who was a Russian agent: a man too old to be my cousin but just the right age to be my uncle: the professor."

"What do you mean?"

Georg jumped up and began pacing about the terrace. "Why would Buchanan have asked me if my cousin was in fact my uncle? Because he knew there was a man of that age in the Russian secret service who was involved with the helicopter deal. If he hadn't known that, he wouldn't have had any reason to ask. The only other reason would be his having a weird sense of humor—his way of telling me that he thought my cousin story was nonsense. But I don't think that was the case. I'm not saying my story about the cousin was particularly convincing. But I don't think Buchanan regarded it as nonsense. Not to mention that I don't think Buchanan had such a weird sense of humor. So the bottom line is that he knew there was a man from the KGB who was old enough to be my uncle and who was involved in the helicopter matter. How did he know?" Georg stopped pacing up and down the terrace and looked at me challengingly.

I began to see his point. "Because he . . ."

"Because he knew him!" Georg cut in. "Buchanan knew him because the other seller wasn't Joe, but the professor. The two must have met at some point, and though they wouldn't have exchanged business cards, Buchanan recognized the professor. And he knew that the professor would recognize him too."

"Furthermore, he knew that he and the professor didn't have the appointment you spoke about on the phone," I added, "and regardless of how you sounded on the phone, it was clear you weren't the professor."

"So something was wrong," Georg said, "and to figure out what was wrong, Buchanan went to the airport. And suddenly Joe turned up!"

"And he suspected that Joe had heard about Buchanan's offer to the Russians and was about to expose him. So he wiped the slate clean: no Joe, no professor, no traces, no evidence."

Georg stood there with his hands in his pockets, looking out over the ocean. He didn't say anything for a while. Then he spoke again. "I was really thrown for a loop. Not because of all Buchanan's shady dealings at the expense of Gorgefield Aircraft, but because of how I tended to overlook critical issues and ignore them, thinking they were just insignificant details."

"Do you have a specific detail in mind?"

"Helen told me once," Georg began, but then turned and looked at me. "You know all the details, you wrote them down. Why should I go over it all again?" He went to the table and raised his glass. "To Joe Benton!" We drank, and he refilled our glasses. "And to the nameless professor, who tried to teach me how to cut through the Gordian knot." He sat down. "I reread the story about Alexander the Great and the Gordian knot. It was just as the professor said: many had tried to unravel the knot, but Alexander simply cut through it with his sword. Whoever was to unravel the knot would rule Asia, and the promise came true for Alexander. And yet he fell ill in Asia and died. You see, he ought to have tried untying the knot. All knots can be untied, because we are the ones who tie them." Georg smiled at me. "There are no Gordian knots, just Gordian ribbons."